I Hate My Life 6

By

Dr. Kenton E.C.

THIS IS A WORK OF FICTION. NAMES, CHARACTER, PLACES AND INCIDENTS ARE EITHER THE PRODUCT OF THE AUTHOR'S IMAGINATION OR ARE USED FICTITIOUSLY, AND ANY RESEMBLANCE TO ACTUAL PERSONS, LIVING OR DEAD, BUSINESS ESTABLISHMENTS, EVENTS OR LOCALES IS ENTIRELY COINCIDENTAL.

COPYRIGHT

Dammit. Tonight, of all nights.

I was under no mistaken illusions that there would be no more complications for us, but seeing Josh standing next to mom caught me completely off guard. Had she invited him or had he shown up on his own?

I turned back to Sharon, her smile gone. I briefly caught her eyes and she looked almost panicked. I had just enough time to gently s□ueeze her elbow, trying to reassure her, before Max came to us.

"Jimmie, may I borrow your sister for a moment?"

Her head swung around to look at Max, sending her hair flying behind her.

I bent down and whispered to her, "Don't worry, I'll be right here."

If I had been any further away, I wouldn't have been able to hear her response, "Okay."

I nodded to Max and forced a tight smile before he held out his arm in front of Sharon, directing her towards a group of tables on the opposite side of the room from where our friends and family were.

She took a few steps before I could see her visibly collect herself. She pulled her shoulders back, lifted her head, and walked with more confidence as she approached the tables.

I stood there like a moron, dumbfounded, but impressed with how Quickly she turned on the charm for whoever Max had wanted her to speak with.

When I saw that she was okay for the moment, I turned towards mom and walked to the table. My eyes flickered from person to person. Maria and Mia were both wide-eyed and Mia was covering her mouth. Jeff had his arms crossed in front of his chest and while his head never moved, his eyes moved back and forth between myself and the side where Josh was standing.

Before I could completely close the distance, mom stepped towards me. We stopped together about five feet from the table and she gave me a Quick hug before staying close to speak Quietly with me.

"Can we go outside for a minute?"

"Yeah," was all I could say.

I held out Sharon's violin and things for Jeff, who took them from me, briefly grasping my forearm and nodding. I followed mom out into the hall and we walked a bit down the hall to give us some more space in case anyone came to or left the reception.

"Jimmie, I didn't know Josh was going to be here. I wouldn't do that to Savannah and it's not my place, but she's told me so little and Josh and I talked for a bit after I saw him here."

"What did he say?"

"Max invited him."

I rubbed my eyes, s☐ueezing the bridge of my nose. Dammit. Max didn't know any better. All he knew was that Sharon and Josh had been in a relationship and played together for even longer, then it suddenly ended and had repercussions for the music program.

I sighed.

"Jimmie, I asked Josh what happened between him and Savannah."

My throat closed.

"All he would say was that they hadn't spoken since New Year's. I told him that I knew he had proposed and she had said no. He wouldn't tell me why. Jimmie, what the hell happened?"

Shit. Sharon and I needed to tell her, we were going to tell her tonight, but together. Think fast, Jimmie, one issue at a time.

"Mom, Sharon and I have talked, but I think she needs to be here for this conversation."

"Why? What's going on?"

"I need you to just be patient. This is all going to get sorted out tonight, I promise. Let's go inside and sit down for a bit."

I turned to go back to the reception, but she reached out and grabbed my arm.

"Jimmie, is everything okay? I'm just worried..."

"Everything is fine, I promise. Let's go be there for Sharon now."

I held out my arm towards the door, trying to encourage her to go back inside. She looked at me, entirely unconvinced, but did head back. We had only been gone for a few minutes.

Sharon was standing next to Max with a group of people. She turned her head to the side and our eyes met. She was struggling to maintain a smile, but I smiled as broadly as I could at her and mouthed,

"I love you," which caused her to noticeably relax.

I went and sat next to Jeff and Mia, across the table from mom and Josh. Josh had his chair turned mostly away from the table and towards mom. I could see that he was watching Sharon as she moved about the room. Mom periodically leaned over and whispered something to him, but I couldn't tell what she was saying. Jeff, Mia, Maria and I made small talk, consciously aware of the awkwardness of the situation.

I watched as Sharon finally made her way to our table. Even in her somewhat delicate emotional state, she was absolutely gorgeous, perfect in every way. I wasn't the only person in the room, male or female, who was watching her every movement.

Mom got up to hug Sharon first. "Savannah, I'm so proud of you."

Sharon then came around to our side of the table and took turns hugging Jeff, Mia, and Maria, responding to their compliments.

She came to me and hesitated. I saw her glance quickly at Josh. I understood, or at least thought I did. I'd been in his shoes not too long ago, watching the woman I loved in the arms of another man. I reached out and grasped her forearm lightly, more leaning to her than fully hugging her. I leaned just close enough and towards the side of her that was away from the table that I could quietly whisper in her ear, "I love you," before quickly backing away.

She looked up at me through her eyelashes and said smiled softly. "Thank you."

Sharon moved away from me and around the table to Josh. He stood up to face her, but made no move towards her. Her back was to me and I couldn't hear, but she seemed to ask him if he wanted to talk. I held my breath as she walked out of the room with him following.

Jeff tried to distract me with some shop talk about NASA while Mia and Maria chatted with mom. I wasn't paying

attention to anything, however, as my eyes were locked on the door, waiting for her to return.

I waited an eternity.

The door opened and Josh came in, but Sharon wasn't behind him.

Josh walked to our table and nodded politely at the rest of us. Mom looked up at him, apprehensive? Anticipating something? He leaned down and gave her a ꓓuick hug, then turned and left. She watched him and then her eyes focused on me. What else could I do? I half-shrugged and mouthed, "I don't know."

Max must have noticed Sharon's absence, because he broke away from a conversation and came to us.

"Have you seen Savannah? There are more guests that would like to speak with her."

I immediately stood up, actually jarring the table a bit.

"She stepped out for a minute, but I'll go look for her."

Mom shot me a look, but I couldn't tell what she was thinking, other than it wasn't her usual supportive smile. I didn't expect to see that for □uite some time after what would be said tonight.

In the hallway, I looked left and right, but didn't see her. I wandered towards the main entrance, but didn't find her there, either.

I paused briefly, noticing the signs for her performance in the lobby. There was a picture of her on stage, wearing a black dress that I hadn't seen before. It must have been from one of her performances while I was gone. She was gorgeous and I could almost hear her playing.

I had a thought and went towards the hall she had performed in earlier in the evening. I □uietly opened the door and went inside, stepping out of the small entry and into the main hall.

Sharon was sitting on the edge of the stage.

She looked up and saw me. I could see tears on her cheeks as I slowly approached her. I sat next to her and she immediately slid next to me. She wrapped her arm around mine and leaned on me.

"You okay?"

She tilted her head up to me and I leaned down, pressing my lips softly to hers.

"I will be. I love you, Jimmie."

We sat Quietly together.

I wanted to ask her what had happened, but it was her choice of whether or when she wanted to tell me. I knew her well enough to know that the only thing she needed right now was for me to be there for her. I rested my cheek on the top of her head and closed my eyes.

After some time, she slid off of the stage and stood in front of me. She took my hands in hers and smiled softly at me.

"I'm going to marry you."

I moved to my feet and took her in my arms.

"Yes, you are, because you are the love of my life and that's the only way it can be."

Her fingers intertwined with mine and we walked out of the hall together, back to the reception.

That had been an unexpected and difficult conversation for her, but we were rapidly approaching the most difficult conversation of the evening. At least now we'd be together.

As we approached the door to the reception, I loosened my fingers to let go of her hand, but she held me tightly. Her beautiful eyes looked up at me.

"It's okay."

"I love you"

"I love you, too."

I smiled at her and pushed open the door. We walked in together.

Every eye in the room turned to see her as she walked in. Her forced smile from earlier in the evening was replaced by her perfect smile that I loved so much.

In the center of the room, surrounded by tables on all sides, she stopped and I stood next to her. She looked up at me and stood on her toes. Even with all of those people around, when I looked at her, she was all I could see.

She kissed me.

It was a light and tender kiss, but her lips pressed to mine and with that, she had announced our relationship to the world. As she pulled away from me, her eyes glistened in the lights with the smallest hint of tears, but tears of joy. She was telling

me with her actions that there was nothing that would ever come between us. Everything we would ever do would be together.

Max took a step toward us from where he had been standing next to our table, with a look of complete shock on his face. Sharon held out her left hand to him, clearly showing her ring. He froze in his tracks.

Every table in the room, except for one, burst into applause. All they knew was that Savannah, the incredibly talented and beautiful violinist that had enraptured the University of Maryland, even beyond the normal music scene, had just effectively announced her engagement on the evening of her solo performance, on Valentine's Day.

At one table, there was only stunned silence.

That single moment lasted a lifetime.

Once the shock had worn off, maybe a second later, Jeff quickly stood and

applauded us. Mia had briefly covered her face before fanning herself with her hands and wiping away tears. Maria simply sat and smiled at us.

Max's shock was replaced with a smile, even if it looked slightly forced and tight. He closed the distance to us with his long strides and took Sharon's hand before placing a light kiss on it. When he stepped to the side, I could finally see mom.

She sat completely motionless, with tears streaming down her face. They were not tears of happiness.

Perhaps five seconds after Sharon had kissed me and shown her ring to Max, and therefore the entire reception, we were enveloped by people offering both of us their congratulations. Even with heels, Sharon may have reached only 5'3" and □uickly lost sight of our friends and mom through the crowd. I could see over enough people that I never lost sight of her as she sat in silence, crying.

I tried to follow Sharon as she introduced me and thanked everyone.

"This is Jimmie, my fiancé."

"Oh, thank you so much. This is my fiancé, Jimmie."

"He proposed earlier today. I played for him tonight."

Every few moments, she would gently reach up and brush her slender fingers along my cheek. The love in her eyes and the touch of her skin washed away all of the trepidation of the evening.

I rested my left hand on her hip as I shook as many hands as I could. Eventually, Jeff was standing before us. I let go of Sharon for long enough for him to hug her and then he turned to me and smiled.

"Tell me the day and I'm there."

He slapped me on the shoulder and embraced me.

As soon as he stepped to the side, Mia was there to replace him, wiping away tears. She hugged both of us at the same time.

"I love both of you. I can't wait to be at your wedding."

Maria was next and showed her own feelings for us in her ☐uiet way.

As people started to return to their seats or filter out of the room, Max briefly took me aside.

"Jimmie, I have to admit, I'm shocked."

"Max, I know how important you are to Sharon. You've been a tremendous mentor to her. I'm sorry we didn't tell you sooner. I hope you can understand."

"I do understand." His voice dropped so softly that I had to lean a bit closer to hear him. "And don't worry, I won't tell anyone that she is your adopted sister. That's not my business."

While I knew he was trying to be kind, that sent a sharp pang through me. He had specified that she was my adopted sister and it hit hard that very few people would tolerate, much less understand, the true nature of our relationship. It would be our secret, to be shared with only our most loved friends and family.

He boomed again, "Congratulations, Jimmie," as he vigorously shook my hand.

By the time I returned to Sharon, the reception had dwindled to a few lingering groups of people. Max quickly moved around, walking with various people as they left the hall. Sharon and I said our goodbyes to our friends.

Eventually, it was just Sharon, Max, mom, and myself left in the room.

Mom hadn't moved in the probably 20 minutes since Sharon and I had stood in the middle of the room and kissed. She hadn't even wiped her face.

Max started to take a step towards her, but Sharon reached out and took his hand, stopping him. She pulled and walked towards the door with him. They stepped outside.

I slowly walked towards mom. Her eyes followed me.

I sat down next to her.

"Mom..."

She turned her head to fully face me. Her voice was steely cold.

"Jimmie... how could you?"

"Mom... we love each other."

"She was happy again. She had moved on from... your mistake. How could you?"

What the fuck? She blamed me for this. As if there was something to be blamed for. I had felt compassionate towards her, sympathetic to the shock that this must be

for her, but that was suddenly replaced with anger.

I wasn't going to play her game, though. I wouldn't tell her that I had resigned myself to a life of regret and sorrow, that Sharon came to me and rescued me. I wouldn't give her even the slightest excuse to blame Sharon. If she wanted to be angry, she could be angry at me.

"This is real, mom, and it's going to happen. She is the love of my life and I am the love of her life. We tried living apart... and it would never work. We have to be together."

Her voice rose, "You're going to ru..."

She stopped as the door opened and her head shot around to see Sharon come in. She didn't finish her thought. Sharon walked towards us, her head low and her hair falling softly around her shoulders.

She sat next to me, taking my hand and interlocking our fingers. Mom stared at our

hands and her ring before looking back at the two of us.

Her voice was harsh. I could understand shock, confusion, even sorrow, knowing that her children were in love and engaged. I couldn't abide her ire, though.

"You can't do this."

Before I could respond, Sharon squeezed my hand and spoke, quietly but firmly.

"Mom, we love you. We would love to have your blessing... but we're not going to ask for your permission."

"Sharon, what did he do? Is this why you and Josh broke up?"

"Jimmie didn't do anything wrong, mom. The only thing he's ever done, for my entire life, is love and support me."

"But Josh..."

"I wasn't meant to be with him. Jimmie is the only one for me. I can't live my life without him."

"Sharon, this will ruin your life. You can't do this. He's your... your... brother."

That caused Sharon's voice to rise and show more anger of her own. "No! I won't let you say that. I almost ruined my life when I pushed Jimmie away. I was shocked when you told us, but I love him. I love him more because he's my brother."

"You don't know what you're saying... this is wrong."

"It's not wrong to follow our hearts, mom."

"I can't... I can't be a part of this." The resignation in her voice, that she was going to choose to not be a part of our lives rather than see us happy, cut like a knife.

Sharon was starting to tremble.

"Mom, I want you in our life. I want you there on our wedding day. Please... be happy for us. Celebrate with us."

Mom barely whispered her response, "I can't... no... this is wrong..."

She had been so still for so long that when she suddenly stood, it stunned both of us.

"When you stop this, I'll be there for you, but I won't be a part of this."

Sharon's body shook next to me.

"Mom..."

I turned to Sharon and pulled her to me, wrapping my arms tightly around her as she broke down and sobbed into my chest. I didn't even care when I heard the door close behind mom as she left, I simply clenched my jaw against the anger inside me.

All I cared about in the world was Sharon. I held her to me.

She was still crying, albeit more softly, when I heard the door open. She lifted her head and we both looked to see who it was. A janitor pulled in a cart and said that he needed to lock up for the night.

I looked back at Sharon and kissed her forehead. She s□ueezed her eyes shut and a few more tears flowed before she said softly, "Let's go home."

We kept our promise to each other that no matter what happened, we would go home together.

At home, our home, Sharon was still in shock from mom's behavior. When we walked in, we went immediately to our bedroom and I sat her on our bed. I gathered sleeping clothes for her and stood in front of her by the bed.

I lifted her to me and hugged her, then unzipped her dress and let it fall to her feet. I pulled her sweatshirt over her head and then lifted each foot into her sweatpants and pulled them up.

I held her in my arms briefly, and then carefully set her down on the bed, pulling the covers over her. I changed from my suit and slid into bed next to her. She cried in my arms until she fell asleep.

I could understand that it would be difficult for mom to accept our love, but for her to completely shut us out...

We spent the next three days together. Every time she cried, it broke my heart and my anger for mom built. I took care of her the only way I knew how: be there for her and hold her. Physically, I made sure that she ate and slept as much as she could.

On the third day, we each received an email from mom. Sharon asked me to read hers with her.

Mom apologized for her reaction at the reception, but said that she was trying to do what was best for us. She was completely convinced that Sharon and I getting married would ruin our lives. She tried to explain that she wasn't angry at us, but still couldn't support us.

Her email to me included much of the same thoughts, but was blunter, concluding with the message that it was my "obligation to be the adult and see what the right thing to do was."

After we finished reading and sat processing for a few minutes, Sharon spoke first.

"Jimmie, I want you to respond for both of us."

"Okay..."

"She has a choice: she can support us and be a part of our life or she can believe we're making a mistake and not be a part of our life. Whenever she is ready to accept and support us, we'll invite her back, but until then, she is not welcome to sit and judge us."

I sat at my desk and wrote carefully, but kept that message. Before clicking send, I sighed deeply and Sharon reached around me from behind and hugged me.

"You're all I need, Jimmie. I love you."

"I am yours. I love you, too."

———————

Spring came to Maryland, as it always does, chasing the frigid air of winter away. As the trees and grass turned green and the campuses, both Maryland and NASA, came to life, Sharon and I spent more and more time outside. Every weekend that it didn't rain, we walked over to the Mall and sat by the fountain.

The first week after Sharon's concert, we took some relatively simple steps to decouple our lives from relying on mom. Sharon closed her bank account that mom had used to transfer money for her rent and living expenses and we opened a joint account together. Since her scholarship now covered all of her educational expenses, we didn't have to worry about tuition payments or making any changes with the school other than to update her permanent address to our apartment. Deep

inside, I hoped that it would send the message to mom about our commitment to each other, that we were entirely serious about spending our lives together.

At the end of February, I attended a therapy session with Sharon and Dr. Vargas. Initially, I was nervous about how open Sharon was about our relationship, since I didn't know Dr. Vargas, but it was clear that they had a rapport with each other built over some two years.

My first impression was that she was trying to determine the nature of our relationship, even if I had somehow coerced Sharon into being with me, but Sharon was always quick to answer any questions that even hinted at that and make it clear that she initiated the original relationship and our reconstituted relationship.

Once that was firmly established, we spoke extensively about mom. It was tough on both of us that we had to cut mom out of our lives the way we did. She had always been there for us, during our best and worst times, but as we made the most

important decision of our lives, she had failed us.

At times, Sharon blamed herself for the way that we announced our engagement after her performance, but I didn't think that mom would have accepted us either way. I understood that there is an incredibly powerful cultural taboo against our relationship, but that didn't mean it didn't hurt. At least the anger had faded and now we both mostly just felt sadness.

We both received periodic emails from her, always saying the same thing. She felt bad for her reaction the night of the performance, but she only wants what's best for us. Our reply was always the same, too. We hoped that she would come to our wedding and share in our love.

Still, as distressing as the rending apart of our family was, Sharon and I had each other. We also had our friends, who had been like family before, but now were our entire family.

We always did our best at home to make sure Maria never felt like a third wheel. In fact, odd as it may seem, it was perfectly natural for us to have her spending time with us. She seemed to have no concerns about sitting in the living room with us while we watched TV and cuddled together. I got to see what Sharon had often raved about when Maria brought food from her family's home. A few times, we joined her for family gatherings and had wonderful times being so welcomed into their home.

I think we both would have spent some time every day with Jeff and Mia if we could. Sharon and Mia often went off on their own while Jeff and I played a round of golf or just bummed around on a weekend. During the week, the four of us had long email chains, joking with each other or talking about various things that were going on.

As long as Sharon and I were together, we were happy.

In late March, Sharon and I were enjoying a warm, lazy morning. We laid naked in bed, drinking coffee and eating muffins as the warm spring breeze carried in the wonderful aroma of fresh grass and flowers through our open window.

As we ate, we inevitably dropped crumbs and I would bend down, gently using my lips to pick up any crumbs I could find that landed on her wonderful skin, leaving a trail of kisses across her belly and supple breasts before sitting up.

At times, I found myself sitting and staring at this incredible woman lying beside me until she would reach up and carefully stroke my cheek with her delicate fingers. As she reached up to me one more time, I caught her hand and held it in mine before kissing her ring.

"Sharon, I love you."

She beamed her wonderful smile back at me. "I love you, too."

"I've been thinking..."

"About?"

"I don't want to wait."

"For?"

"To marry you. I don't want to wait until after you graduate or after I get my master's. There will always be something next, whether it's school, a job, or whatever. It's just... whatever is next, will always be with you. Whatever is next, I want you to be my wife when it happens. Let's get married this summer, or even this spring... as soon as possible."

She pulled me down to her and kissed me deeply.

Gradually, our kiss became increasingly passionate and she pulled me tightly to her, until her breasts were pressed firmly against my chest. She rolled to her back and spread her legs. I stayed with her, moving until I was laying gently on top of her. Our lips never broke contact.

I could feel her hips gently thrust up against me and my now rigid member was resting against her opening, almost begging to be thrust inside. But first, I wanted to take care of her.

I broke our kiss and trailed my lips along her chin, around to her ear, and whispered, "I love you," before lightly kissing down her neck and around her collarbone. I slid my tongue out from between my lips and traced a small trail across her smooth skin until I approached her nipple. I drew circles around her nipple, feeling the slightly bumpy skin of her areola giving gently under the soft pressure of my tongue.

Her nipple stood erect, a beautiful dark brown against the creamy tan of her skin. I sucked it into my mouth, pinching it between my lips and flicking my tongue back and forth across the very tip.

While my lips and tongue took turns working on her spectacular breasts and nipples, I traced the contours of her impeccable body with my fingertips. From her arms and down her sides, feeling the

swell of her breasts give way to her petite waist. My hands drifted further each path up and down her body, across her hip bone and around to the ample curve of her rear, then along the front of her thighs, tracing the line where her leg met her pelvis.

I took my time, savoring the taste and feel of her skin wherever I touched her, with my tongue, my lips, my fingers, or my body. Eventually, I left her perfect nipples behind, kissing down into the valley between her breasts and then along her belly. I placed a kiss on her belly button and briefly thought to myself that someday, she would be the mother of my children.

As my lips explored lower, her hands came to the back of my head and gently tickled the soft hair at the nape of my neck. She had this way of just barely touching the hair with the tips of her fingers, sending shivers down my neck and to my spine.

I felt her soft pubic hair against my chin and could start to smell the sweet musk of her body as arousal took control of her. My

tongue flicked out, lightly licking the creamy skin of her thighs on either side, her hips pushing towards me as I did so.

I wanted to tease her for longer, but I simply couldn't resist. With one long, slow motion, my tongue made contact with the bottom of her very moist slit and licked all the way up until I pressed on the firm bud of her clitoris. A quiet, long moan escaped from Sharon and I looked up to see her eyes closed and mouth open.

She always tasted incredible to me and I greedily lapped at her juices. I flattened my tongue to collect as much of her as I could as I licked along her opening and then used just the tip to swirl around and flick across her clit. This wasn't about teasing, this was about bringing her to release and feeling her body lose control.

Her thighs squeezed against my head as I worked her, alternating between hard and soft, firm and gentle. I used my hands to protect myself, to keep her from completely suffocating me. Her own hands were moving back and forth between my

head, pulling my hair a little before releasing and grasping more firmly onto the sheets.

I rested my hand on her chest, between her breasts, and felt both her breathing and her heartbeat increasing in pace. Just a little more... I pulled her clit between my lips, sucking hard enough that my jaw strained while my tongue flicked back and forth across the little nub as fast as I could.

"Ohhhhhhhhhh," she moaned loudly as her thighs pinched against my head. She climaxed and her wetness on my face as her body went completely rigid. Through her entire orgasm, I continued sucking on her clit, refusing to let up on the pressure.

I pulled my hand down from her breasts and traced my finger along her soaked lips, wetting my skin.

Slowly, I pushed my finger inside of her, never losing any contact between my lips and her clit.

"Oh... ugh..." She was incomprehensible, which was exactly my goal.

I pulled my finger out just as slowly.

"Good... so good," she cooed.

Before she could come down from her orgasm, I pushed two fingers back into her, her body easily, which greedily accepted them. I curled both of my fingers up and rubbed against the tender area inside of her that shared the same nerves as her clitoris, still being licked and sucked on in my mouth.

She whimpered as her body was completely overwhelmed.

I released her clitoris from my mouth and relaxed my fingers inside of her. I felt her body relax slightly as I let up on her. I counted to three in my head.

At the count of three, I lunged back towards her and took her clit in my mouth again, furiously pressing my tongue against her with more pressure than ever. My

fingers straightened and curled inside of her, probing every part of her vagina.

I felt another flood of wetness as her body tensed again. She groaned loudly as another orgasm crashed into her.

I could feel her muscles rapidly contracting around my fingers and she struggled to break contact and relieve the stimulation on her, but I held my arm tightly around her thigh to prevent her from escaping.

"No, no... too much," she groaned.

She tried to push me away with her hands, but I wasn't going to be deterred. One more, I thought to myself. I knew that I didn't need to do anything different, just keep up the pressure on her and inside her.

I straightened my fingers until they were as far inside as I could reach, then pressed them firmly up against the ceiling of her vagina, before curling them back towards her opening.

My mouth was firmly attached to her and I sucked her clit between my lips, until I could ever so lightly pull it between my teeth. I rotated between using my lips, my teeth, and my tongue to stimulate her, trying to provide contrasting sensations every few seconds.

Her head jerked to the side and she shrieked ⬜uickly before a loud moan escaped her lips. Her hips jerked away from me and my lips lost contact for a moment before locking back onto her. Her juices rushed down my fingers, buried inside her, soaking my hand and the sheet below.

Her petite body writhed on the bed. As soon as I let go of her and withdrew my fingers, she turned on her side and curled into a ball. I worried that I had pushed her too far and moved up behind her, pressing my chest to her back, as she struggled to recover.

"Sharon... are you okay?"

I watched her delicate hands, clenching into fists.

After a few minutes, she turned and faced me. She reached behind my head and pulled me to her until her tongue parted my lips and thrust against my own.

When she finally broke away from our kiss, her eyes locked onto mine and the corners of her mouth turned slightly up.

"You will do that to me again."

"Oh really?" I teased her.

"Yes. I demand it. But now, I need something different..."

Her voice trailed off and I watched her body as she rose to her hands and knees. I expected her to move over me to her favorite position, but she didn't, she stayed beside me. I took my eyes off of her body just long enough to see her smile devilishly at me. She wiggled her hips, shaking her rear.

I needed no second invitation.

I pushed myself up and crawled behind her. Her butt formed a perfectly shaped heart from her narrow waist around to where her labia was swollen and glistening. I kissed the small of her back, then back and forth I kissed down each of cheeks until my nose was pressed against her wet opening again. I took one last long taste of her wonderful juices, eliciting a low moan from her.

I couldn't wait any longer, though, and positioned myself behind her. I took my member, hard as titanium, in my hand and touched the tip against her lips. She was so wet and ready for me, that without any pressure at all, the head slipped inside. She pushed her hips back before I could even react and half of my shaft was inside her, too.

With one thrust, I was completely enveloped by her. My hips were pressed against her rear and I could feel pressure on the head of my penis as I bottomed out inside her. I had to s☐ueeze around the

base of my shaft just to keep from finishing right there.

I took a moment to let my eyes drift along her body. Her long hair hung to either side of her head, leaving her flawless back completely bare. Her skin was an incredible honeyed tan and I could make out just the hint of her breasts peeking out from either side. My hands instinctively went to her svelte waist, pressing my palms against her supple skin and grasping her firmly with my fingers.

I slowly withdrew until I was completely out of her. My erection stuck straight out in front of me and needed no guidance to press against her again. I easily slid back inside, eliciting a groan of approval from both of us as her wetness and tightness encompassed me.

I began rhythmically withdrawing and thrusting back into her, watching myself disappear inside of my Sharon. Each time I entered her, she thrust her hips back against me until the flesh of her rear and my hips slapped together.

I wanted her to have her pleasure though. I let go of her hip and reached around her, between her legs, until my finger found her hard little clit. After sliding down to wet my finger on the mixture of her juices and my pre-cum, I pressed my fingertip against her clit.

"Yesssss..." she hissed at me.

I slid my other hand up from her hip and cupped her breast, pressing my palm against her firm nipple, and pulled her up to me until her back was pressed against my chest. Her hair slithered between us and with one shake of her head, much of it flew over my shoulders and cascaded down my back, introducing a new sensation to our lovemaking.

Because of our height difference, I had to move my legs closer together and sit back on my haunches, while she kept her legs outside of mine and rested her rear on my thighs. I hadn't planned it that way, but she suddenly found herself in control again as my thrusting ability was limited in that

position. She used her thighs to lift herself up and then drop herself back down onto me.

I locked my lips onto her neck, sucking and gently nibbling. I let my hand wander across her breasts, cupping one then the other, teasing her nipples, and holding her to me by her taut belly. All the while I vigorously fingered her clit in a race to bring her another orgasm before I couldn't hold back anymore.

I wish I could say that I was some kind of sex god, capable of inhuman feats of sexual stamina. Unfortunately, I am but a man. This incredible creature underneath me, the love of my life and a sexual goddess in her own right, wouldn't allow that, at least not until I was entirely spent and she could use me as she pleased.

With each bounce on me, she grunted and s□uealed. The bed was now creaking beneath us, bearing the impact of our weight driving down into the mattress through my knees. Her □uickening pace was going to break me.

She pulled off of me one more time and slammed down with enough force to send a small jolt of pain through my body.

"Unnnnnngggggg..."

She let out a guttural groan of pleasure and I felt wetness run down my shaft, coating my balls and thighs. With her orgasm, I couldn't hold back any more and came inside her with a loud groan of my own. I lost count of the spasms racing through me as I released spurt after spurt.

We collapsed forward in a heap on the bed in a tangle of hair, arms, legs, and bodies. I □uickly lost consciousness and fell into a restful sleep, much needed after the physical exertion.

I woke up on my side, spooning Sharon as she curled up pressing her back to my chest. I ran my hand along her body, tracing her wonderful curves with my finger. She immediately turned her head back to me and kissed me.

When we broke, she said the words that I live by, "I love you."

I pressed my lips to her ear.

"You know, you didn't answer my □uestion."

She quickly turned back to look at me again.

"I didn't?"

"Well, it wasn't so much a □uestion as a re□uest."

Her eyes flickered back and forth on mine. She had forgotten what we were talking about before our love making.

"I don't want to wait. I want to marry you this year... as soon as possible, even."

Now she turned her entire body to face me and pressed her forehead to mine. I could feel her warm breath on my lips as she whispered to me.

"Yes."

____

Our wedding would be May 31, the second weekend after the end of the semester. It would give us enough time to plan and invite friends, as well as a short buffer from the end of classes.

We reveled in making our preparations together, deciding on a location, guest list, and various other necessary things to do.

One of the most important tasks was to determine the legality of our marriage. We would go through with the ceremony either way, as nothing would keep us apart, but we wanted to look into if there was a way for us to be legally married in the eyes of the state.

Our first step was to take a trip to Norfolk, where Sharon was born. At the records office, we reΩuested a copy of her birth certificate. What it said would determine whether we could proceed or not. When the clerk returned with a legal copy of her birth

certificate, Sharon clasped her hands to her mouth.

The birth certificate reported a file number, Sharon's full name using her mother's maiden name, her place of birth as Norfolk, and her mother's information. It was the most information she had ever learned about her mother.

For her, our, father's information, there was nothing.

Outside of her adoption records, which were sealed as her adoption occurred prior to 2000, there was nothing that we needed to present in order to get a marriage certificate that would tie us together as adoptive siblings, much less half-brother and half-sister.

We drove to Williamsburg that afternoon, walking along the living history street hand in hand, before eating dinner outside on a beautiful spring evening. That night, we made love, one step closer to being husband and wife.

Back at home, after a maddening amount of frustrating research, we were unable to unambiguously figure out if Maryland would view adoptive siblings getting married as a criminal act.

The strongest indication one way or the other was a memo from the assistant Attorney General in 1989, which included the most important words we had ever read: "In conclusion, Family Law Article, S2-202 does not prohibit a marriage between a man and a woman related as brother and sister solely by reason of adoption."

From the establishment of the law in 1777 until 1984, adoptive relationships were considered e□uivalent to consanguinity. However, in 1984, Maryland updated the Family Law Article, separating blood and legal relationships.

We decided that it was a risk we were willing to take.

A week later, we were preparing our invitations for our relatively limited guest list.

"Sharon, I'm just about done here, but I think we should do one more."

"For who?"

"Mom."

She looked up at me, her face clouded over and her eyes were full of sadness. She walked to me and stood behind me, setting a blank invitation in front of me before wrapping her arms around my shoulders. She held me while I filled out the invitation.

I didn't know if mom would reply, much less come. I hoped that when she saw the invitation, it would be the clearest demonstration that with or without her support we were going to be together forever. Maybe, just maybe, that would break through the wall she had built between us with her... reservations.

The next morning, Sharon held my hand as I carried the invitations to the mailbox and dropped them in. I turned to her and we kissed.

Throughout the rest of the spring, we continued with our lives. It seemed like every minute of the past two and a half years, there had been some kind of weight on our shoulders. For the first time, it felt like we were almost care free. Setting a date for our wedding gave us a certain sense of freedom.

Sharon continued giving concerts, albeit with less fre□uency. She only gave two during the semester after her Valentine's performance, despite massive demand for more shows. She performed with the orchestra once and with piano accompaniment as a fundraiser for the school.

There were some protestations from Max about the reduced load, but in the end she convinced him that all would be well and she'd return to a more regular performance schedule in the fall. Between her increased

biology coursework and planning for our wedding, she was reaching the limit of hours in a day.

For the first time in my career, I was a co-author on a paper published in a scientific journal. Goddard often takes a backseat to the more visible NASA centers around the country, whether it's the Jet Propulsion Laboratory in California or the home of the astronaut corps in Houston. The work we had been doing on the Van Allen belts resulted in a nice publicity boost for the excellent work that Goddard does.

Despite all of this, the times we treasured most were when we set aside work, music, school, and even wedding plans. We delighted in simply being together.

There were nights when we walked in the cool evening air to our special places around campus. We could sit and talk for hours or I would simply hold her in my arms while we watched the world go by. When it got late, we'd walk home, hand in hand, and make love.

Other nights, we did the things that we had always dreamed of doing together.

In April, Sharon and I went to our first Opening Day at Camden Yards. She was absolutely adorable, wearing tight khaki shorts, a fitted orange Orioles t-shirt, and her favorite Orioles hat on a beautifully clear day. We never stopped holding hands as she cuddled against me for the duration of the game. After a thrilling walk-off win, we made our way home.

She talked for the entire drive, recalling the game in vivid detail. Close pitches she thought were called the wrong way. Inconse☐uential two out singles. All of it. She was reliving the tenth inning when we walked into our bedroom.

I took her in my arms and slowly lifted her t-shirt over her head, revealing her perfect breasts. She rarely wore a bra, not needing the support and seeming to revel in catching my eyes focusing on her perky nipples poking through the thin fabric of whatever shirt or dress she was wearing.

I moved down her body, placing small kisses between her breasts and over her belly. As I fell to my knees, I unbuttoned her shorts and slid them down, along with her panties.

She stood before me naked. Flawless.

She stepped backwards until she was against the bed, then sat down.

"Are you coming?"

I ripped my shirt over my head and struggled out of my shorts without even unbuttoning them. In moments, I was laying next to her in bed, placing delicate kisses along her body.

"Make love to me." She was completely intoxicating when she commanded me. It was my weakness and she knew it.

I moved back up her body from where I had been nuzzling her breasts. She immediately reached down and I felt her slender fingers around my erection, guiding me to her. She rubbed my head up and

down. I could feel her wetness lubricating me.

When she stopped and held me against her, I pushed my hips forward and my head slid inside. I carefully and gently pushed further, seeking her warmth. After a few thrusts, I was fully enveloped.

My mouth found hers and we kissed as I laid still inside her. When she reached down and grasped my butt with her hands, I withdrew slightly and thrust back into her. What started as short, shallow strokes, evolved into longer, slower, sensual lovemaking.

I could feel her body moving under me. She rolled her hips against me, changing the angles each time I pushed fully into her.

We moved against each other, her soft skin touching my body from the tips of her fingers tracing my back, to her thighs pinching against my hips.

I listened to the sounds of her soft moans as her body responded to mine. I withdrew and slid back into her in rhythm with her breathing, our bodies synchronizing to each other.

When Sharon pressed her lips to my ear and whispered, "I love you," I groaned and released myself inside her.

There were times when we let ourselves go in bed, exhausting each other before collapsing thoroughly satisfied. Yet, when we made slow, sweet love, we were equally satisfied, having shared ourselves completely.

———————————

The Bay Bridge faded behind us as Sharon and I drove back to the Eastern Shore. In less than twenty-four hours, she would finally be my wife.

We checked in at our hotel and I waited patiently at the hotel bar while Sharon changed upstairs for our rehearsal dinner. When she arrived, every head in the room

turned to watch her walk in. From top to bottom, she was immaculate.

Her hair was pulled back in a twist behind her shoulders, falling down among her remaining free hair, which flowed behind her. She had on just the slightest bit of makeup, her natural beauty outshining anything and everything.

She wore a ruby red sundress, with spaghetti straps over her shoulders, and a moderate V in front, revealing an alluring amount of cleavage. The bodice clung tightly to her petite frame, with a lace pattern tying above her waist, revealing little windows to her caramel skin. The dress hung loosely over her hips and rear, flowing down to her knees. She wore simple black sandals with low heels.

The second she took my hand, everyone in the bar seemed to exhale, as if they had been holding their breath at the sight of this incredible woman. I leaned close to kiss her.

I held my cheek close to her and said ☐uietly, "You're absolutely incredible."

Her loving smile was all the response I needed.

I texted Jeff to let him know that we were on our way to the restaurant and would be there in five minutes. He was waiting out front for us when we arrived.

I got out and went around the truck, opening the door for Sharon and taking her hand in mine to help her down. I watched in awe as she slid out of the truck, her dress riding up and revealing her silky smooth thighs, before falling back to her knees as her feet hit the ground.

Before going inside, Jeff smiled warmly as he greeted us both with hugs. Few people knew as much about us, what we had been through, as Jeff. Inside, Sharon and I paused for a moment while Jeff went into our reserved room first. I held her in my arms until we heard applause. We walked in together, her hand in mine.

Inside, two dozen of our most loved friends stood for us as we walked to our seats at the front of the room.

The evening was absolutely incredible. We thanked everyone profusely for sharing in such a special event with us. We ate a spectacular dinner of blue crab and flounder, sweet corn and other local vegetables.

While we ate, a slideshow that Mia had prepared with pictures of Sharon and I, from childhood to just a few weeks before our wedding, ran on a television screen on the wall. I felt a brief pang of guilt when the picture of me in Marseilles, the Mediterranean in the background, slid by, but I knew that for better or worse, our time apart was a part of who we were.

I was leaning over and kissing Sharon's cheek when she squeezed my leg, hard.

"Ow!"

"Jimmie..." She gasped more than she spoke.

"Sharon, what is it?"

Before she could answer, I felt a hand on my shoulder. I turned to see Jeff, the smile gone from his face. He nodded and I followed the direction of his gaze.

Standing just inside the door was mom.

I froze as about a hundred conflicting emotions surged through me.

Sharon started to rise from her chair, but I pressed on her thigh to keep her seated.

"Let me."

I was going to find out what mom was doing here before letting her speak to Sharon. I wouldn't let her say a single thing that would take away from this weekend for Sharon. I stood up and walked around the table, s☐ueezing Sharon's shoulder gently before I was out of reach. Mia moved to my seat, so that Sharon was sitting between her and Maria.

I watched mom's face as I approached her. I couldn't read her, but I could see her blink hard, forcing a tear down her cheek. I held out my arm, directing her towards the door. The conversation we needed to have couldn't happen in front of everyone.

Mom looked up at me, fearful.

I kept my voice low and calm. "I'm not asking you to leave. We need to talk outside."

She turned and I followed her through the door. Outside she faced me.

"Mom. Why are you here?"

"Jimmie, I'm sorry."

"You've said you're sorry a dozen times, but that doesn't change the fact that you can't be happy for us, can't support us."

"No... no. I really am sorry. I've been selfish. I... I... shouldn't have walked away."

I shifted from one foot to the other. I wasn't in the mood for another lecture on how it was my fault, how I was ruining our lives.

"No mother wants to learn that her children are... in a relationship. It's just... not done. But I shouldn't have put my own distress ahead of the two of you. You're my children and I love you. I'm sorry that I didn't listen to you. I want you to be happy."

"Mom, we are happy... together. It's the only way we can be happy."

"I know. I know now. When I got your invitation, it wasn't just abstract anymore, it was real. You two... you're... family, but you're more. I should have seen it, given you a chance to show me..."

Her voice trailed off and she covered her face with her hands.

"Jimmie, I'm so ashamed. I should have supported you. I failed you both."

She was trying to apologize, but I wanted to be completely clear.

"Mom, do you want us to be happy?"

"Yes."

"Do you see that we are happy together?"

"Yes."

"Do you want to be a part of our lives?"

"Yes. I've missed you."

"Wait here."

I went back to the door and went inside. Mia and Maria were both leaning close to Sharon. Her eyes were already on me. I moved to her, giving her a small smile. When I was next to her, I took her hand.

"Come with me."

She rose to her feet and stayed close to me as we walked to the door, her entire body pressed against my arm. I pushed open the

door and turned to mom. She was wiping her eyes with a tissue.

Sharon's voice was soft and girlish, full of fear. "Mom..."

"Savannah, honey, I'm so sorry."

Mom broke down in tears.

I leaned to Sharon and whispered in her ear, "It's okay."

I let go of Sharon's hand and she stepped into mom's embrace.

"I'm so sorry, baby girl. I love you. Please forgive me. I want you to be happy. I want you to... be with Jimmie."

We talked for several minutes, mom telling Sharon what she had told me. She would be there for us now and she would support us. Mom hugged both of us and we walked into the dinner together. She sat and cried as pictures of Sharon and I flashed on the screen. We took turns sitting with her and telling her the story of our love.

It was easy for us to welcome mom back into our lives. The pain and anger resulting from her reaction to our engagement, the sadness of having her out of our lives for a few months, wasn't more important than the years she had been there for us. We never wanted to cut her out, but we had to protect ourselves. The minute she could see our love, see what we meant to each other, we welcomed her with open arms.

Our family was whole again.

Two hours later, I sat in the hotel bar with Jeff, nursing a beer.

I had said goodnight to mom, who went back to Salisbury, but promised to be at the wedding.

Sharon and I held each other as we said goodnight, preparing to spend our first night apart since the night before she told me that she still loved me on that cold January day. Given the uniqueness of our marriage, it was kind of odd for us to

choose to honor that tradition, but there it is.

"It's been a long path for you, Jimmie."

I looked over at him and smiled.

"It's just starting for us."

I took a long sip of beer.

"Thanks for being there for us, every step of the way."

He patted me on the shoulder.

I woke up the next morning well before my alarm and watched the sun rise over the Atlantic Ocean. I laid in bed, trying to get a few more hours of sleep, but the excitement coursing through me was too intense. I eventually gave up.

I texted Jeff and he came over to my room, where we sat drinking coffee on the balcony, watching the waves break on the beach below. Around lunchtime, we made our way downstairs and talked over crab

cakes, as various friends filtered through the hotel restaurant and greeted us.

Every time I closed my eyes, even briefly, I tried to picture Sharon walking towards me as I waited for her. I knew, without a doubt, that she would be magnificent.

In the afternoon, I returned to my room to get ready and less than an hour later, Jeff and I were driving south along the coast. We pulled into a parking lot on Assateague Island and spotted two large tents on the beach.

Jeff and I walked together to where Sharon and I would be married. As we passed between the two tents, Jeff stopped and I walked further onto the beach alone. I passed down the aisle between the rows of chairs and to a simple trellis, with white roses woven in the latticework. I crouched down and picked up a handful of sand, letting it flow between my fingers, before writing Sharon's name and smiling to myself.

I stood up and turned to walk back to Jeff. We walked around one tent as he showed me various preparations and we talked about the details of the ceremony. The other tent was where Sharon, Mia, and Maria were getting ready. As I walked past, I touched the canvas of the tent and smiled, thinking how close I was to her.

Guests began to arrive and Jeff hustled around, seating most of them. When mom arrived, I held out my arm and she let me escort her to her seat in the front row. Before I could leave, she held my arm for a moment.

"Jimmie, thank you for letting me be here."

"We want you here mom. We always did. Thank you for coming."

And then I waited.

I stood to the side of one tent, out of view of the guests. It was an incredible day that I couldn't have scripted better, hovering around 80°F with a gentle cool breeze coming off of the water and across the

beach. The azure of the sky melted into the dark blue of the ocean on the horizon.

I thought about the times that I had stood on the beach in Spain, looking out over the sea, wishing that I could have done something, anything, to have Sharon standing next to me. In a few minutes, she would stand next to me and become my wife.

I remembered, with incredibly vivid clarity, the summer after she graduated from high school when we spent almost every minute together. I could see her sitting next to me at a Shorebirds game, her hair spreading out beneath a baseball hat or flying behind her as she jumped up to cheer.

My mind moved forward, to her first day on campus and how the only thing she wanted was to spend that time with me. She fell asleep in my arms and when I drove her to her dorm, she kissed me. That kiss changed my entire world.

I could feel her skin against mine, from the first time we made love to her fingers in

my hand as I slid her ring onto her finger on a cold November night.

I looked down at my feet, half buried in the sand, as I thought about the night we learned the truth about us and the devastating impact on us, on her. It was a part of the path that brought us here, to our wedding day.

I had gone away to try and discover myself again, learn who I would be for the rest of my life. In the end, I had only learned that my life was meaningless without her. She had recovered and even thrived in my absence, though. As much as that hurt, when I had watched her perform, I couldn't contain my adoration of her.

The pain of that time would always be a part of me and I would cherish every second with Sharon more because I had felt what my life would be like without her, the indescribable suffering of losing her.

She had everything and I had nothing.

Until she came back to me. She risked everything that she had worked for to reach down and pick me up, pull me out of the darkness of a life without her. Her love for me rescued me. Somehow, through everything, through all of the changes in our lives, we found each other.

It couldn't be any other way.

Somewhere in the back of my mind, I heard a voice. "Jimmie, are you ready?"

I turned around and Jeff was waiting for me.

"Yeah."

I came around the corner of the tent and saw that all of the seats were filled with our guests. Jeff and I made our way to the front, various friends smiling and laughing as we went. I stopped and bent down to mom, giving her a kiss on the cheek, before taking my place. I shook the hand of our officiant, Nancy.

I turned and waited.

Stepping out of the tent first was one of Sharon's friends from the music program. I had only briefly met her at a reception after one of Sharon's performances with the orchestra, but we had decided that having her play at our wedding would be perfect. Sharon worked with her, arranging a modern song in a classical style.

She took her place to the side and bowed to me before raising her violin and playing "All of Me".

As soon as the music started, the tent opened again and Mia stepped out wearing a beautiful gold bridesmaid dress. She began walking slowly down the aisle between the seats. A few feet after her, Maria appeared and followed her.

I held my breath, waiting for my first glimpse of Sharon. Throughout all of our planning, she hadn't let me see her dress or even hinted at its design.

And then she appeared.

How do you describe the love of your life, on the day of your wedding? She is perfection.

Time stopped as she stepped forward into the waning sunlight, the sky to the west behind her now changing into soft oranges and reds. Everyone gasped as she moved down the aisle.

Her bare feet sunk into the sand, obscuring her brightly painted red toenails.

Her dress was pure white, standing in stark contrast to her dark hair and caramel skin. The cut itself was simple, strapless and formed to her body, only slightly loosening around her hips. It was cut down below her knees at tea length and flowed gently as she walked, hanging slightly lower in the back than in the front.

The material was absolutely spectacular. Over an inner layer of satin, lace was intricately woven in and out, crossing back and forth, for the entire length of her dress. It was complex, elegant, and spectacular.

Her hair was entirely free and formed a veil behind her as it blew softly in the breeze. A wreath of white flowers sat atop her head. She wore a blue sapphire pendant around her neck and carried a bouquet of white calla lilies clasped in her hands at her waist.

And of course, that smile. Every part of her was smiling, from her lips stretched wide revealing her perfect white teeth to her wonderful dark eyes.

She was entirely flawless. She is my Sharon, my love.

She reached me and I held out my hand for her, her fingers sliding gracefully into mine. She handed her bouquet to Maria and we turned until we were facing each other and the ocean. I couldn't stop myself from lightly rubbing her fingers, tracing the outlines with my fingertips.

I couldn't take my eyes off of her and I could barely hear the words being spoken as our ceremony started.

"Friends and family, thank you for coming today to celebrate in the marriage of Michael and Savannah. You have gathered here to share in their commitment to each other and to offer your love and support as they begin their lives together, as husband and wife.

"Every person travels a unique path in life, seeking meaning and purpose, affection and companionship. Our paths are often filled with successes and failures, both of which create who we are as individuals and eventually contribute to who we become as partners.

"Michael's path has taken him from his home here on the Eastern Shore, to incredible successes in education, his career, and life. He has traveled across the ocean and into the farthest reaches of the universe inquiring into a deeper knowledge of the world around us and an understanding of the significance of life. He will continue exploring in the years and decades to come, yet he will always return

home, to where his heart belongs, with Savannah.

"Savannah's path has carried her from the shy girl of her youth to the incredible woman that stands before you today. Her life has been defined by the interweaving of her love for science and her passion for music. She has achieved the highest honors in education and dazzled audiences with the enthusiasm for life that she expresses through her violin. Wherever she may go, to concert halls around the world or a laboratory here in Maryland, she will continue bringing together the elements of life that she loves, with Michael by her side.

"For Michael and Savannah, their paths, as incredible and beautiful as they have been apart, could only ever lead to each other and to the joining of their lives into a single path forward, together.

"In making this formal commitment, Michael and Savannah pledge to each other and to you that throughout friendship and faults, companionship and struggle, their love will serve as a guiding influence,

forever bringing them together, always on a single path.

"And now, Michael and Savannah would like to make their vows to each other, for all here to witness."

Sharon turned to me, her eyes glistening, and took both of my hands in hers. When she spoke, her voice □uivered as she fought to hold back tears.

"Jimmie..."

She s□ueezed my hands.

"... my dear Jimmie. You are the love of my life and my inspiration. Every day I live is a day that I seek your love and friendship. Everything that we have been through has made us into the people that we are today and I accept all of it without any reservation, because I now stand before you on our wedding day.

"I will always be by your side, providing you joy and comfort. I pledge to you my

love and support, for every day of my life..."

I smiled at her. I knew there was more, but her voice was breaking apart and she couldn't continue.

She finished with a whispered, "I love you," and she s☐ueezed her eyes shut, forcing tears down her beautiful cheeks. I brought her hands to me and lightly kissed them. She opened her eyes and smiled through her tears.

"My wonderful Sharon. You are absolutely everything to me and all that I need in the world. I live and die with your smile and your touch. I need you beside me for the rest of my life, as my best friend... my companion.

"I am overwhelmed when I think about the ways that our relationship has changed over the years, all of the experiences that we have shared and the times when you rescued me from my absolute darkest moments. I was completely lost without you and I am so incredibly thankful that

you have chosen to spend your life with me.

"The only thing that can possibly compare to my love for you is my admiration for the incredible person you have become. I am in complete awe of all that you are, my perfect Sharon. Every part of me strives to ensure that I never disappoint you, that I never let you down in any way.

"You are the love of my life. I pledge to you my love and support, for every day of my life. I will comfort you and cherish you, protect you and nurture you, always. On this day, I give my life to you. I love you."

I clenched my jaw to hold back my own tears.

Nancy asked softly, "May I have the rings?"

Jeff immediately stepped forward and handed our rings to her.

Her voice rose as she addressed everyone. "These rings will serve as an abiding

symbol of the love and union between Michael and Savannah."

Savannah took my ring and, hands trembling, carefully slid it onto my finger.

I held her ring in my hand for a moment. I had once closed my eyes and cried, thinking of the moments that I had lost, including our wedding. I would never lose another moment with her or have to envision life without her. Now when I closed my eyes, I would only see... our house, our children... our future.

I held her slender hand in mine and slipped her wedding band onto her finger, gently placing it next to her engagement ring.

Nancy spoke again as Sharon and I kept our eyes locked onto each other.

"Savannah, do you take Michael to stand by your side from this day forward, as your lawfully wedded husband?"

Sharon's lips trembled.

"I do."

She smiled through her tears.

"Michael, do you take Savannah to stand by your side from this day forward, as your lawfully wedded wife?"

My voice was strong, for I had never been surer of anything in my life.

"I do."

"I now pronounce you, in the eyes of all here and the State of Maryland, husband and wife. You may..."

And before she could even finish, my arm slid around Sharon's waist and I pulled her to me.

I kissed Sharon, my wife.

I hadn't seen Josh since New Year's Eve in North Carolina. In the few weeks since the spring semester had started, we hadn't run into each other in the performing arts center and had no classes in common.

I had emailed him once in January offering to meet him for lunch if he wanted to talk, but he never responded. I ended up giving the box of his things that I had collected to a mutual friend from ensemble to return to him

Now he was standing next to mom on the day of my engagement to Jimmie.

I froze. What do I do? What do I say? Why is he here now?

My eyes found Jimmie, right next to me. His hand was on my arm and I felt his fingers gently s☐ueeze me.

Behind me, I heard Max.

"Jimmie, may I borrow your sister for a moment?"

I swiveled to look at him. He wasn't smiling, but he had his usual friendly and determined demeanor.

I felt Jimmie's breath on my ear.

"Don't worry, I'll be right here."

I didn't want to step away from him for even a moment, away from the strength that he gave me, but I knew that I had to.

"Okay."

Just that one moment with him comforted me. He would always be there for me, there was no need to worry.

I allowed Max to direct me towards tables with guests. I had done this before and tonight would be no different. I would smile and graciously thank them for their support of both myself and the music program.

Max lead me from table to table as I shook hands with countless people and thanked them for their compliments.

"Savannah, you were absolutely unbelievable. Thank you so much."

"Savannah, you have an incredible future ahead of you."

I tried to ensure that every person had at least a few moments of personal time, but I was constantly trying to position myself so that my eyes could seek out Jimmie. I had lost sight of him for a few minutes and when I tried to find mom, she was gone, too. Were they talking? I wanted to be there when we told her...

Eventually, I saw mom walk into the room, followed by Jimmie. She didn't look overly happy, but she didn't seem to be distraught or upset, either. I immediately doubted that he had told her about us. As he walked behind her, Jimmie focused his eyes on me and smiled broadly.

I could hear him in my mind when his lips formed the words, "I love you."

I smiled back at him.

I love you, too. I want everyone to know.

Jimmie and mom returned to their table while I continued mingling with Max. Every time I caught Jimmie's eye, he smiled at

me and the apprehension I had about the conversations that needed to happen with both Josh and mom melted away. Whenever I wasn't shaking hands with someone, my right hand held my left and I ran my fingers over my ring.

Finally, I had greeted everyone and I could return to my friends and family. I focused on Jimmie as I walked to their table. He sat straight up in his chair, his suit jacket hanging perfectly off of his frame.

Mom rose to greet me first, throwing her arms around me and saying, "Savannah, I'm so proud of you."

I thanked her and received similar compliments from Jeff, Mia, and Maria with hugs of their own. I laughed when Mia said I looked like a model and didn't seem to want to let me go. Maria and I were the same age, so our relationship was more e□ual in a sense, but Mia always seemed to be my proud older sister. I loved both of them and looked forward to asking them to be my bridesmaids.

Then I was next to Jimmie. My instinct was to throw myself into his embrace, but I saw Josh out of the corner of my eye. This couldn't be easy for him and I didn't want to make things any harder. I was fully aware now of the impact I had had on Jimmie when he had to see me with Josh.

Jimmie's hand was on my forearm and I felt his fingertips on my bare skin. I yearned for his touch, always. He leaned close to me and whispered quietly in my ear, "I love you." Even when we were being coy about our relationship with others around, he found little ways to touch my heart with the simplest of gestures.

I wanted to kiss him, but I held myself back. I simply looked up at him and said, "Thank you."

I sighed softly to myself and moved around the table. Josh rose to face me. I felt a wave of guilt, knowing that I had once been the one to bring a lopsided sheepish grin to his face, but now he simply gave me a blank look, devoid of emotion.

"Josh, will you come talk with me?"

He barely nodded.

I turned and headed for the door while Josh followed a few steps behind. In the hallway, there just wasn't enough privacy for what we needed to say, so I Quickly turned to him and said, "Let's go to the hall." Again, his response was just the slightest nod. My heels clicked on the floor and reverberated through the hallway as we walked.

I stepped into the hall where I had just performed while wearing Jimmie's ring. I went to the stage and turned my back before hopping up and sitting on the edge. My hands rested on my lap.

I watched as Josh moved to the edge of the stage, too. He leaned against it, several yards away from where I sat.

I knew what I needed to say, but was trying to figure out the exact words, when he spoke. It was the first time I had heard

his voice since he had walked out of the room after I had broken his heart.

"Savannah, I'm sorry if I startled you. Max asked me to come tonight and I went back and forth on whether or not I should. It was good to see you play again."

We sat quietly for a moment and I collected my thoughts.

"I'm so sorry about what happened."

His Quiet response broke my heart. I looked directly at him, watching all of his reactions. He made steady eye contact with me for the first time.

"I'm sorry that I asked you to leave that night. I shouldn't have. I should have stayed and talked to you."

"You didn't do anything wrong. The last thing I ever wanted to do was hurt you. I had been avoiding everything that had happened with Jimmie for so long, for years, but then when I confronted it..."

"You feel about him the way I feel about you."

I felt my jaw tremble. Oh no, I hope not. I truly hoped that I wasn't the one for him.

"Josh, you'll find someone, someone who can make you happy and will never hurt you, someone you can love and have a beautiful family with."

That had to sound like a horrible, empty platitude to him. I hoped against hope that it was true. He deserved that life. Maybe he and I could have been happy together, but it wasn't meant to be.

"I'll never stop loving you."

"I know. I'll never stop loving you, either. You will always be so special to me. What happens in the future doesn't change or take away the time that we had together, the happiness that you gave me."

His lips were pressed tightly together and tears began running down his face.

"I'll never forgive myself for hurting you, because I want you to be happy."

He wiped the back of his hand along his cheeks. We sat Quietly, with me watching him while he only gave quick glances in my direction. My heart broke for him; he deserved so much better than this.

Finally, he sighed deeply and moved away from the stage, walking to me and standing directly in front of me. He looked down at my hands and saw my ring.

"You're going to marry him."

I ran my fingers over my ring.

"Yes."

"I want you to be happy, too. I wish it were with me, but I want you to have everything you want in life."

Oh Josh... you're such a good person.

He shuffled his feet and his legs were nearly touching my dangling feet. He

leaned forward and I watched as he came closer to me. He softly pressed his lips to my cheek and then stood straight.

His voice was soft, "I love you. Goodbye, Savannah."

"Goodbye, Josh."

I had one brief moment to see the sadness written on his face before he turned away from me. I watched every step until he turned the corner and was out of sight. I closed my eyes and felt tears run down my cheeks as I heard the door open and then swing close, clicking shut.

I would still see him around the music program, even if not in class or ensemble, then possibly just from running into each other in the performing arts center. I knew it would be impossible for us to rebuild any kind of friendship, but if I did see him, I would do my best to be a friendly face.

I sat and cried, remembering so many of the moments that we had together.

After some time, I heard the door open again. I needed the jolt, because it had been long enough that it was time for me to return to the reception.

I looked up to see Jimmie coming towards me. My Jimmie.

Thank you for coming for me.

He walked slowly towards me and I tried to smile just a bit at him. He looked wonderful in his suit and some of my sadness was lifted as I felt the love for him that was so central to who I am.

He sat next to me on the edge of the stage and I pushed myself as close to him as I could before sliding my arm around his and resting my head on his shoulder. Being with him is the single most comforting thing in my life.

He asked me, "You okay?"

I looked up at him, into his beautiful eyes, and he leaned down to kiss me gently.

"I will be."

I will always be okay as long as I have you.

"I love you, Jimmie."

I laid my head on his shoulder again and felt his cheek rest on top of my head. There would be time to tell him what Josh and I had talked about, but for now, I just needed to be near him. I felt my confidence return as the aura of his love surrounded me.

I slipped off the stage and stood before him, sliding my hands around his. I smiled at him.

"I'm going to marry you."

He moved to his feet and enveloped me in his arms.

"Yes, you are, because you are the love of my life and that's the only way it can be."

The only way it can be. From the moment I was brought into his life, this was our

destiny. We have so many choices to make in life, but it was never a choice for me to love him. He would always be everything to me.

My hand found his and our fingers interlocked. We walked together back to the reception.

At the door to the reception room, I felt Jimmie's fingers loosen their grip on me.

No. It's time. It's time for everyone to know about our love, to know that I would be his wife, that everything I do is for him.

I held his hand firmly and looked up at him.

"It's okay," I assured him.

His fingers tightened around mine again and he pushed open the door for me. This moment was everything to me.

As soon as we moved from the mildly lit hallway into the bright reception, I felt the eyes of everyone on me, on us. I lead

Jimmie to the center of the room, never taking my eyes off of him. I stopped and turned to face him as he looked down into my eyes. Everything about him, his kindness, his intelligence, his height and his subtle strength... everything soothed me and gave me confidence. He made me a better person, simply by being with me.

I pulled down on his hand as I stood up on my toes and my lips found his. I kissed him and felt the security of his love.

When I backed away and stood before him, the brief look of shock on his face was immediately replaced by a wonderful smile. I could feel a smile creep across my mouth, spreading to my cheeks, my eyes, and my entire body.

We'll never be apart again.

I saw Jimmie's eyes move to the side and I turned my head to follow his gaze to see Max. Now is the moment.

I held up my left hand towards Max, my ring sparkling in the light. I doubt if it was

shining anywhere near as brightly as I was. I reveled in this moment for Jimmie and I, a moment that took us years to earn.

Suddenly, we were surround by an entire room standing and clapping, not for me as after my performance, but for both Jimmie and I. My head spun, searching the crowd for the smiles of our friends and family, but my eyes kept seeking Jimmie, my Jimmie.

Max reached us and placed a kiss on the back of my hand.

Jimmie and I were ☐uickly enveloped by a crowd of people offering congratulations from all directions. I wanted to introduce everyone to my perfect fiancé, my inspiration. Even as I shook hands and showed my ring, I couldn't help reaching up to touch Jimmie, caressing his cheek with my fingers. He never took his hand off of me, holding my hip or brushing the small of my back, keeping his body firmly next to me.

And then I looked up to see Jeff and Mia. They had been our best friends and then

during our dark times, were rocks for both of us. They were are family and always would be.

The first time Jimmie let even the tiniest bit of space between us was for Jeff to embrace me in his long arms. The moment he released me, Mia was squeezing the both of us tightly.

"I love both of you. I can't wait to be at your wedding."

Mia finally let go of us and I was able to see Maria. She took my hand in hers and ran her fingers over mine, tracing around my ring. She smiled at me. I didn't know what having a twin sister was like, but I could only imagine it was like our relationship. Without saying anything, she conveyed everything to me. When Jimmie and I were married, she would be my maid of honor.

I turned looking for Jimmie and he was speaking quietly with Max. After I heard Max, in his deep bass voice, tell Jimmie,

"Congratulations, Jimmie," they walked to me.

It was only then that I saw mom for the first time since we had come back into the reception, as the room was nearly empty now. She sat completely frozen, her cheeks wet from tears, but she wasn't smiling.

I know mom, I know you're shocked. We'll talk through this and it'll be okay.

Max turned to go to her, probably to congratulate her, but I □uickly reached out to him and pulled him towards me.

He briefly turned to look at mom and I think the realization of her tears and the look on her face hit him. He looked down at me, his smile replaced by concern.

Very □uietly, I said, "Max, we need to talk."

He followed me as I went to the door. Outside, I spoke softly.

"Max, she doesn't know about us and I don't think she'll be happy. Jimmie and I were first engaged more than two years ago. Her response is part of why we broke up."

I could see him beginning to piece together the limited information he had in his head.

"That's why you started playing violin again and why you and Josh..."

I quietly interrupted, "Yes."

"I see, I see. I'm sure this is very difficult for her to process."

"Jimmie and I will need to speak with her. We didn't really mean for her to find out like this, but he proposed today and..."

Max interrupted, "You played that last piece for him."

"Yes."

"It was marvelous. I want you to know that anything you and Jimmie need, I'm here for you."

"Thank you, Max."

He smiled down at me.

"Good night, Savannah... and good luck."

"I'll talk to you soon. Thanks for everything tonight."

He turned and I watched for a moment as he proceeded down the hall towards his office. I sighed and pushed open the door to the reception room.

I barely heard mom as I entered the room.

"... to ru..."

She stopped talking mid-sentence and immediately spun to look at me.

As I approached them, my eyes moved rapidly back and forth between mom's shocked face, still wet with tears, and

Jimmie's tense look. I sat delicately on the seat next to Jimmie and scooted close to him before sliding my hand into his.

When I looked back at mom, her voice was so cold that it sent shivers through my body.

"You can't do this."

Yes, we can mom.

I collected myself and pulled Jimmie's hand onto my lap.

"Mom, we love you. We would love to have your blessing..."

Please, mom, be happy for us. See our love.

"... but we're not going to ask for your permission."

Whether she approved or not, my life would only ever be with Jimmie by my side.

"Sharon, what did he do? Is this why you and Josh broke up?"

I knew how much she cared about Josh and it was easy to see why. He was so polite and kind to her. Yes, Josh and I couldn't be together because I'm meant to be with Jimmie, but what did Jimmie do? I tried to speak calmly, pushing down the anger that was boiling up inside me. She wasn't going to blame him for us.

"Jimmie didn't do anything wrong, mom. The only thing he's ever done, for my entire life, is love and support me."

And that's what you've done for me, too, mom. Please don't stop now.

Her voice was softer, "But Josh..."

"I wasn't meant to be with him. Jimmie is the only one for me. I can't live my life without him."

Again, her tone turned to anger and accusation, "Sharon, this will ruin your life.

You can't do this. He's your... your... brother."

I lost control and my anger took over. I wouldn't let her say that.

"No! I won't let you say that. I almost ruined my life when I pushed Jimmie away. I was shocked when you told us, but I love him. I love him more because he's my brother."

Mom seemed briefly taken aback at my response, "You don't know what you're saying... this is wrong."

I do know what I'm saying. This isn't your choice and you can't judge us.

"It's not wrong to follow our hearts, mom."

And then she terrified me with her response.

"I can't... I can't be a part of this."

Mom? Please, please understand us! You can be there for us, with us.

"Mom, I want you in our life. I want you there on our wedding day. Please... be happy for us. Celebrate with us."

You need to be there when we get married. You need to be there for me and for us.

"I can't... no... this is wrong..."

My body tensed when she suddenly put her hands on the table and pushed herself quickly to her feet. The anger, the sadness, all emotion left her voice. She spoke as if she were stating a simple fact.

"When you stop this, I'll be there for you, but I won't be a part of this."

No... no... don't go...

Jimmie pulled me to him as my world began to collapse again. He held my waist tightly while stroking my hair and I sobbed uncontrollably.

Mom...

I was startled when I heard a voice that I didn't recognize.

"I'm sorry, but I need to lock up in here."

I looked up to Jimmie and he pressed his lips to my forehead, gently kissing me. I looked into his eyes.

He was the only family I had left now.

"Let's go home."

I was barely aware of anything that happened until Jimmie and I were laying in bed, his arms providing as much comfort as I was capable of feeling. I fell asleep with the echo of his voice in my mind, "I love you, Sharon. You are my everything."

His strength was all that kept me going for days until finally she contacted us.

I watched as Jimmie read an email from her, a grimace on his face. I asked him to hold me while I read her email to me. It didn't matter if she was sorry for how she had reacted at the reception, she had made

her decision... and we had made ours. Nothing would ever tear us apart; we are one and that is how we would respond.

"Jimmie, I want you to respond for both of us."

"Okay..."

I drew on his strength.

"She has a choice: she can support us and be a part of our life or she can believe we're making a mistake and not be a part of our life. Whenever she is ready to accept and support us, we'll invite her back, but until then, she is not welcome to sit and judge us."

As Jimmie typed our answer to her, I stood behind him and wrapped my arms around his shoulders, squeezing myself tightly to him with my cheek pressed to his ear.

Mom had once said to me, "It's just the way it had to be." She was right, but not in the way she thought. If she couldn't love

us, accept us, and support us, then this was the way it had to be.

"You're all I need, Jimmie. I love you."

He pressed his cheek to mine as I continued to hold him.

"I am yours. I love you, too."

____

Jimmie and I were unconditionally there for each other, providing the strength and support that we both so desperately needed. There were days when my devastation at mom's reaction overwhelmed me and Jimmie would hold me as I cried. There were days when Jimmie seemed consumed with sadness and I would curl up next to him, sharing the warmth of my body.

Still, we couldn't dwell on the decision that she had made. We had our lives to live.

The first week after Valentine's Day, we had lunch with Jeff and Mia. We explained

what had happened with mom, much to Mia's dismay. Jeff, as with all things, took it in stride it seemed. They were incredibly supportive of us, as always, and I was thankful to have them. Maria was also saddened by mom's decision to not support us. The three of us would sit in the living room and Maria and I would talk while Jimmie mostly sat and listened.

They were our family now.

Near the end of February, Jimmie joined me to meet Dr. Vargas. Initially, she seemed reluctant to fully embrace Jimmie and I could understand her concerns about an older brother and younger sister being in a relationship, but eventually I was able to assure her that he is everything to me and my path forward will always be with him. The conversation shifted and we talked about mom and her reaction. At the end of our time together, Jimmie stepped outside and Dr. Vargas hugged me, telling me that she was proud of how I was taking more control in my life, rather than letting situations dictate to me.

Jimmie and I both continued to receive emails from mom, but her judgment never changed and neither did our decision. The only two choices were to accept us or not be in our lives.

We were at peace with our decision and when the moments of sadness passed, we basked in our love for each other. After classes and work were handled for the day, Jimmie would take me into his arms and we would be together, happy.

On the last weekend of the month, a late snowstorm blew through and shut down everything for several days. We bundled up in ski clothes and enjoyed a different perspective of a place that was so central to who we are.

As we walked to our spot on the Mall, where he had proposed, I stepped where stairs should have been, but immediately sunk almost to my shoulders in a snow drift. Jimmie looked down at me and laughed, before jumping in next to me and kissing me while we lay buried in snow.

When we got home, we went to bed and warmed our bodies together.

As much as I looked forward to the moments that I knew would come for us - graduation, our wedding, a home - I enjoyed the simple moments that we had together, whether it was laying in the snow as he kissed me or the look on his face when he set down dinner on the table as I studied. I remembered the first time he put his arm around me and how natural it felt. I couldn't have even imagined then just how we would develop together, as if we were each an extension of the other's body.

In many ways, we lived as if we were already married. While we existed in that somewhat transitional place, myself in college and him progressing through his master's and at work, every passing day felt less and less like we were starting to build a life together. We weren't starting our future anymore, we were living it.

I imagine that if one experienced the exact same happiness at all times, you'd □uickly

become immune to it and everything would become boring after awhile. I can only describe my happiness with Jimmie as twinkling, constantly radiating and pulsing in different styles and intensities.

In March, Jimmie continued finding ways to surprise me and build my anticipation for the future moments we would have.

On a warm spring morning, we lay in bed, enjoying another moment together that would become a pleasant memory for us.

Jimmie took my hand in his and kissed my ring.

"Sharon, I love you."

As many times as he said those words to me, they always felt like he was telling me for the first time, sending a pleasant glow throughout my body.

"I love you, too."

He looked incredibly pensive as his eyes held mine.

"I've been thinking..."

My curiosity peaked.

"About?"

"I don't want to wait."

"For?"

"To marry you. I don't want to wait until after you graduate or after I get my master's. There will always be something next, whether it's school, a job, or whatever. It's just... whatever is next, will always be with you. Whatever is next, I want you to be my wife when it happens."

Oh, Jimmie. I love you more than you can possible know. Of course I want to marry you as soon as possible, this minute if we could. All that is next for me is you.

"Let's get married this summer, or even this spring... as soon as possible."

Yes, yes, a thousand times yes!

My hand slid behind his head and I pulled him down to me, kissing him, feeling this wonderful man who would be my husband. He couldn't wait to marry me and I couldn't wait to be his wife.

We made wonderful, passionate love to each other, him bringing me to so much pleasure that my mind and body gave out.

Afterwards, we slept, with his body wrapped around mine, my back pressed to his chest.

He spoke ☐uietly, "You know, you didn't answer my ☐uestion."

I couldn't even remember what we had talked about before we had made love.

"I didn't?"

"Well, it wasn't so much a ☐uestion as a re☐uest."

I searched, trying to remember.

"I don't want to wait. I want to marry you this year... as soon as possible, even."

Whatever is next... we'll always be together.

I turned to face him and pressed my forehead to his. I had everything I wanted in life in my arms.

"Yes."

We began planning the wedding immediately. He promised me the world, but all I really wanted was to stand next to him and say, "I do."

We briefly discussed getting married on campus, but eventually we decided that as much as we loved the University of Maryland, we couldn't see ourselves getting married anywhere other than the Eastern Shore. The school was an intrinsic part of us, the place where we found our love for each other and after we had been separated, rediscovered ourselves together

again, but the Eastern Shore is home and it always will be.

Once we settled on a date, May 31, we knew exactly where we wanted to be married. It was a beautiful time of year, just before the full heat and humidity of summer set in, and on a beach beside the ocean was where we would exchange rings.

In April, Maria, Mia, and I spent a Saturday shopping for dresses in Annapolis. It was almost absurdly easy to find their bridesmaids dresses. I didn't want to be the bride who puts her best friends in something horrific, so the three of us worked together to pick out beautiful gold dresses in a light summery style.

My dress was more of a challenge. I waivered back and forth and I must have tried on dozens of dresses before narrowing the selection to two.

The first was a full length gown, with a strap that wrapped up from the chest and around my neck. The bodice was tight and the back had a large ribbon laced from my

shoulder blades to my rear, giving a very corset-like appearance. The gown spread around me, forming a large pool of fabric that moved in ripples behind me as I walked. It was a very traditional look.

The second was a light-weight sundress which very few people would have mistaken for a wedding gown. However, it would be absolutely perfect for a warm afternoon wedding on the beach. Two thin spaghetti straps went over my shoulders and a modest neck in the front revealed only a small amount of cleavage. The skirt was cut at my knees and I could see it blowing softly in the breeze. Despite its non-traditional appearance, it was very elegant.

I waivered back and forth, trying on each dress several times.

When I had changed back into my own clothes and come out of the dressing room to discuss the decision with Mia and Maria, only Mia was there. A few moments later, Maria came up to me and tapped me on the shoulder. When turned around, she was

holding the dress that I would be married in. She had found it for me.

It was perfect the moment I laid eyes on it, an incredible combination of traditional elegance and modern simplicity. I tried it on for Maria and Mia.

The dress was strapless and about half of my back was bare. The cut was simple, clinging tightly to my chest, belly, and hips, before loosening around my thighs and flowing to tea length halfway down my calves. The material was actually two layers, an inner layer of silk, keeping the modern look, while a layer of lace was intricately woven from top to bottom.

As soon as I stepped out of the dressing room, Mia was nearly in tears and even Maria was uncharacteristically emotional.

I stood still while the seamstress took measurements for the final adjustments, trying to hold back my own emotions, thinking about standing on the beach. I could close my eyes and picture the ocean,

the sand, and Jimmie standing next to me with his gorgeous blue and green eyes.

The magnitude of that moment overtook me and I began crying with tears of joy.

The following week, after my mid-terms, Jimmie and I left early on Friday to go to Norfolk, to find out as much about my past as we could and if we could be legally married.

At the records office, I showed the clerk my driver's license and submitted the request for an official copy of my birth certificate. I don't know what I was hoping for, other than to see nothing that would stand in our way. The wait was excruciating, giving my mind too much time to dream up horrible scenarios.

The clerk finally returned and set my birth certificate on the counter in front of me. I stared at the information about my birth mother, information that I had never asked our mom for fear of hurting her. Her name was Angelica and she was only 22 when

she had me. I wondered if I would be a mother at that age, in less than two years.

My eyes continued reading, but where my father's information should have been, the form was blank.

I looked up at Jimmie and he smiled at me.

We left the records office holding hands and while he said he wanted to do a bit more research, I knew that nothing would keep us apart. We would be married, even in the eyes of the State of Maryland.

We got onto the highway and I held his hand as we drove with the windows down, enjoying the beautiful spring weather. Within an hour, we were exiting the highway and I looked over at Jimmie.

"Oh, getting gas."

I raised an eyebrow, knowing that we had gotten gas in Norfolk and still probably had 3/4 of a tank left, but I quickly smiled when I saw the signs for Colonial Williamsburg. Shortly after, we parked and

were walking along Duke of Gloucester through the living history area.

Jimmie's hand found mine and he smiled at me.

"I just wanted to spend some time with you."

I squeezed his hand and pressed my body against his arm as my heart and mind were lost in my love for him.

We walked in and out of various little shops and museums, with Jimmie insisting on buying me a pair of silver earrings in one store and a number of handmade candies in another.

As we sat and ate dinner outside, Jimmie tapped me on the arm and pointed in the direction of an actress, "You know, you would have made an awfully attractive serving wench." I giggled at him and used my hands to lift my breasts, greatly exagerrating the cleavage at the top of my t-shirt.

"Oh, you mean like this?"

His eyes nearly bugged out of his head as they dropped down to take in the view.

I teased him some more, picking up his beer and thrusting my chest forward while taking on what I imagined to be a colonial accent, "Would you like some more mead, sir?"

His eyes finally made their way back up to mine.

"Feeling a bit saucy tonight, are ya?"

"Maybe..." I let my voice trail off with quite a bit of implied meaning.

We sat and talked, laughing and flirting for hours.

We'd never really had the pursuit phase of a relationship, so it was fun to in some small way experience the subtle changes in voice, the wandering eyes, or the almost inadvertant touches that you hope will lead to so much more.

Of course, instead of the trepidation of a first date or fears of saying something wrong early in a budding relationship, we were completely at ease and after Jimmie paid the check, his arm slid around my waist as we walked together.

It was dark when we got back to his truck. He opened the door for me and held my hand as I climbed in. I took the moment to brush my fingers along his chin, one of my favorite activities.

We were barely on the road for a few minutes when he turned into the driveway of a beautiful white colonial house with perfectly manicured grounds.

"Jimmie..."

Again, his response was the same, "I just wanted to spend time with you."

As soon as he had parked and opened my door for me, I threw myself into his arms.

"I love you."

"I love you, too."

"Jimmie, can we afford this?"

"Don't worry, everything is okay."

When I let go of him, he reached into the back seat and pulled out a bag. I walked next to him, with his hand resting on the small of my back, gently guiding me.

Inside, the bed and breakfast was incredible, decorated in a traditional American colonial style. The owner greeted us with tremendous cheer and showed us to our room after a □uick tour of the premises.

Our room was massive with an incredible four-post bed dominating the center. Small chairs were placed at a table under the window. I walked to the bed and rested my hands on the end, feeling the softness of the □uilt and bedding. Before I could turn around to thank him for another wonderful surprise, I felt his hand on my waist and then his body pressing against my back.

He pulled my hair to one side and his lips were pressed against my neck, sending goosebumps and shivers shooting through my body. I tilted my head to the side to give him better access and he traced his lips down to my shoulder and then back up to my ear in a slow, winding path.

I moaned when his hips pressed against my rear and I could feel his erection through his jeans. He continued kissing my neck and I ground myself back against him. I waited with anticipation as I felt his fingers pull my hair to the other side of my neck and were soon followed by his lips on my skin again.

I cooed softly, "Jimmie..."

I let him seduce me this way for several minutes, before turning to face him. I reached behind his head, pulling him down to me and letting my tongue dance across his lips. In moments, he was kissing me passionately and our tongues were in full contact, pressing against and massaging each other.

I put my hand on his hips, then slid them up to his chest and began unbuttoning his shirt. I could feel his lean muscles through the fabric. As soon as I reached the last button, I pulled it away from his body and let it fall down his arms.

As soon as I could, I let my lips wander, pulling away from his mouth and kissing his chin, then his neck, and down to his chest. I felt his soft hair as I moved back and forth across his pecs, alternating between short, glancing kisses and lightly sucking on his skin.

Meanwhile, my hands continued the work of undressing him, unbuckling his belt and unbuttoning his jeans. I moved my fingers to his hips and slid them inside the waist of his pants and boxers. As my hands pushed down from his hips to his thighs, his pants and boxers followed.

While taking off his pants, I found myself looking straight at his member, standing proudly in front of him. I had felt it in my fingers so many times, but rarely got a

very close look. I was almost shocked that something that large could fit inside me. As I rose back to my feet, I let my fingertips lightly brush him and then rubbed my breasts against his erection.

He moaned quietly and I thought to myself, "You have no idea what I have planned for you."

It was my turn to seduce him.

I held his hips and coerced him into turning his back to the bed, then pressed on his chest to force him to sit.

I moved until I was a few feet away from him, then lifted my finger to my lips and gently held it between my teeth, looking at him through my eyelashes.

My hands dropped until they rested at my waist. I unbuttoned my jeans and pulled them open just enough to reveal a tantalizing glimpse of my black panties. I slid my thumbs into my jeans and pulled down a few inches, revealing a bit more for him.

His face was frozen, eyes locked on me, and just the tiniest hint of a grin on his lips.

I stopped and tilted my head to the side and let the corners of my mouth turn the slightest bit upward, too, then I turned until my back was facing him. I looked over my shoulder at him, out of the corner of my eye, my face partially obscured by my hair.

Again I hooked my thumbs into my jeans and pushed down until I could feel the change in temperature on my rear as just my panties remained. I thrust my butt out just a bit and pushed further until I felt my jeans give away and fall to my feet.

I stepped out of them, having not taken my eyes off of him the entire time. I watched as his eyes traveled up and down my body and his tongue lightly wet his lips.

I turned back and faced him in my tight t-shirt and panties. My eyes took in the scene, with him leaning back on his hands on the bed, his member standing tall above

him, and then they drifted down towards my body, where my nipples were clearly poking through the material of my shirt. I continued with my silent strip tease for him.

Don't you dare take your eyes off me...

My fingers moved back and forth across my hips, inching my shirt above my waist, then above my belly button. As my shirt reached the bottom of my breasts, my smile spread wider and I held my finger in the air at him, taunting him.

Again, I turned away from him. I continued pulling my shirt up, my nipples feeling the cool air in the room and becoming even firmer as they were uncovered. My hair rushed through my shirt and fell down my now bare back. I slowly extended my arm away from my body, letting my shirt dangle for a moment before dropping it. I could feel my hair brushing against the top of my rear.

My hands slid down my body and found the edge of my panties. I pulled gently and felt

every inch as my skin was slowly exposed to the air. When my butt was halfway uncovered, I looked over my shoulder and Jimmie's mouth was hanging open.

I pushed and felt my now thoroughly saturated panties pull away from where that had been clinging tightly to my lips. A few more inches and they too fell to the ground.

I stood naked, my back to Jimmie.

I slowly turned to face him and watched his eyes as they grew bigger and roamed across my body.

He began to push himself back to sitting straight up and looked like he wanted to stand and take me into his arms, but I pursed my lips and again held my finger straight in the air at him and moved it slowly back and forth. He immediately froze.

No, no... this is my game.

I moved to him, one slow step at a time until my legs were pressed against the edge of the bed. His knees brushed against my hips.

My hands reached out and rested on his thighs, pushing them apart until they were no longer against me.

I slid my hands down to the bed beside him, removing our last point of contact, and paused, looking directly into his eyes. The look of shock was exactly what I wanted.

Leaning forward, I lowered my head and watched as my hair fell over my shoulders and brushed against the bare skin of his legs. I leaned further and dragged my hair up his body, across his member and to his chest.

He sighed as he exhaled for the first time in what felt like minutes.

I looked up and my hair now formed a curtain between us. When I reached out and brushed a finger along the underside of

his member, tracing the length of his shaft until tapping the small opening at the tip and pulling away, his body jerked at the contact.

My head moved lower and I paused just above him, letting my breath run across the head of his member. My lips pressed against his skin and he jerked again under me. Lower again and my tongue slid out from between my lips, touching the very base of his shaft and slowly licking his entire length.

I listened as he drew in a □uick breath and held it. It was time.

My lips parted and I took his head into my mouth. My tongue swirled around, tasting every bit of him. I sucked more of him into me and my tongue could feel the ridge between his head and shaft, tracing circles around it. I moved as far as I could, until about half of him was inside my mouth. I wanted to take all of him, but I just couldn't manage it.

My lips formed a seal against his skin and I began sucking gently. Slowly I pulled back until I released him. Again, I took him into my mouth. My hand reached up and my fingers wrapped around the base of his erection, holding him steady for me.

Every time I pulled his wonderful erection into my mouth, I let my tongue dance circles around it before releasing him. My fingers gently pumped as I bobbed my head up and down on him.

I counted time in my head. One, I pulled him into my mouth. Two, I ran my tongue around him. Three, I took as much of him as I could and sucked gently. Four, I released him.

Slowly, I increased my tempo, with my lips, my tongue, and my hand.

"Sharon..."

A small smile came to my lips before I moved down again and took a bit more of him as I adjusted to feeling him in my mouth, pressing lightly against my throat.

His voice became more urgent, "Sharon..."

One. Two. Three. Four. A bit more ⬚uickly now. A bit more pressure with my fingers and my lips.

"Sharon..." It was more of a moan than an actual word.

My saliva leaked down his shaft and my fingers spread it around him, using it for lubrication.

"Ohhhh..."

Yes, I'm ready.

I reached up with my other hand and formed a small cup, before lifting until I made contact with him. I barely applied any pressure at all, knowing how sensitive he would be there.

"Sharon... I'm gonna..."

I pumped faster, sucked harder, and swirled my tongue more furiously.

Right as I released him from my lips, I felt his legs tense beside me. I immediately locked my mouth back onto him, holding his head between my lips and sucking so hard my cheeks hurt.

And then I felt it, the first spurt as he came in my mouth. I swallowed , the salty, and even a bit sweet fluid, as □uickly as I could. He groaned above me and my fingers continued pumping him while I held my mouth still, milking the last drops from his body.

Eventually, I felt no more and swallowed the last bit before pulling away from him. I stood up and pulled my hair back behind my shoulders so that I could see him, his chest rapidly expanding and contracting, his eyes half-closed.

When his eyes focused on me, he gasped, "Oh, Sharon..."

I smiled at him and said nothing while slowly backing away. Again, he started to sit up and again I used my finger to warn

him to be still. He needed to rest and I needed my own release.

I continued backing away until I was just in front of one of the chairs next to the window. I sat down, and turned my body until I was completely facing him. I held my finger to my lips, shushing him before he could say anything.

Slowly, I traced a line with my finger, down from my lips to my neck, between my breasts, and across my flat belly. I felt my soft pubic hair and slouched slightly in the chair, spreading my legs as I moved down.

Again Jimmie's jaw dropped.

I felt my first convulsion as my finger traced across the edges of my incredibly moist lips. I reached down until I was at the very base of my opening and gently probed inside, feeling my wetness coat my finger. I pulled up and moaned softly, feeling the entire length of my slit. When my finger brushed against my clit, I felt my second convulsion.

I gently pressed against that oh-so-sensitive spot and my hips involuntarily thrust, seeking more contact. Slowly, I moved my finger back and forth, spreading my wetness.

It wouldn't be very long at all...

I had my last glimpse of Jimmie, leaning back on the bed watching me, before my eyes closed and I slid my finger inside me. My legs straightened with another convulsion and I struggled to keep myself upright.

I spread my legs further, intending on giving Jimmie a show that he would never forget.

I slid a second finger inside and began slowly pumping them in and out. My other hand wandered to my breasts, taking a nipple between two fingers and lightly pinching before releasing and moving to the other.

I could feel the pressure building inside as my convulsions became more intense,

more urgent. I moaned as my fingers moved more rapidly. I imagined Jimmie's fingers inside me, pleasuring me.

"Ughhhh..."

I groaned. I was so close... so close.

I thrust my fingers into myself faster, more vigorously.

My thumb moved away from my fingers that were inside me and sought out my clit pressing on it firmly.

I pressed harder on my clit and thrust my fingers as far inside as I could reach.

My body went rigid and my orgasm slammed into me. I felt my juices running down and over my hand. My mouth hung open in a silent scream and pleasure shot through every nerve in my body.

After several moments, I felt my fingers slide out of me and my eyes slowly opened to see Jimmie, his hand wrapped around

his once again erect member, slowly stroking himself.

Oh no, no, no. That's mine.

I pushed myself to my feet, my knees slightly weak as I wasn't fully recovered from my climax. I went to the bed and reached out, pulling his hand away from what I wanted.

I climbed up onto the bed, placing a knee on either side of his thighs, holding myself above him. Reaching between my legs, I wrapped my fingers around his member and lowered myself onto him, pressing him against me. I easily slid onto him, as I was still soaking from my orgasm, and my body responded to that wonderful feeling of him filling me, opening to receive all of him.

His arms slid around my back and he pulled me to him, my chest and belly pressing against his, feeling his warm body. My hips naturally rolled, forcing him into me at varying angles.

I looked down, into his eyes, and his lips pressed against mine. We kissed deeply and passionately as I ground my hips on to him, sending unbelievable stimulation through my body.

Perspiration began building on my neck, running down my breasts and between our bodies. My hair cascaded down my back and over his arms.

I alternated between grinding my hips hard on to him, gently rolling back and forth, and lifting myself almost completely off of him before thrusting back down onto him.

Every sensation I was feeling was hitting every part of my body. I could feel him inside me, from my toes to my fingers and everywhere in between.

We reached such a pace that I couldn't hold my lips to his anymore. I leaned back, my hair sliding across my bare skin, and he buried his face between my breasts.

I need you to cum. I'm going to lose control and I want to climax with you. Please, hurry... I can't hold on.

His hands slid down to my rear, taking a cheek in each hand and helping me as I repeatedly impaled myself on him. He squeezed my rear tightly and pulled me down roughly onto him one last time, hitting the deepest parts of me.

He groaned and I felt him release his seed inside me. The first shot sent me over the edge and my arms clutched at him, scratching his back as another climax overtook me. I felt every convulsion of his orgasm inside me, filling me.

We held each other, panting and struggling for air, until our lips met again. Our kiss gradually softened until we could breathe again, our hearts quietly slowing as one.

"My Jimmie... my Jimmie..."

"I love you, Sharon. I am yours."

I fell asleep in his arms, as always, but with visions of our future together running through my mind as I lost consciousness.

The next morning, we showered together and got dressed. We were often ☐uiet after such intense lovemaking, letting our physical love dominate for a time.

The smallest touches between us - his hand on my hip as I brushed my hair or a soft kiss on my neck as I buttoned my jeans - said everything that needed to be said. We belonged to each other in every way.

Jimmie took our bag out to the truck, before returning to settle the bill with the owner. I waited, sitting on the swing on the front porch. When he came out, he held out his hand and I slid my fingers into his. He had a funny smile on his face.

"What're you grinning about?"

"This..."

He handed me a piece of paper.

I unfolded it and looked at our bill. The total was crossed out and next to it was a note.

"I saw your lovely lady's engagement ring, but no wedding rings. Congratulations on your upcoming marriage." A little heart was drawn at the end.

I looked up at Jimmie and his grin was now a full smile. My only response was to press myself tightly to him, to the love of my life.

____

In many ways, the weeks before our wedding passed so quickly, but as my anticipation built, as the reality of the preparations washed over me, the days passed more and more slowly. I needed to be his wife, more than I needed air and water.

As the end of the semester approached, we had less and less time to spend those moments together, worrying about nothing except each other.

We often found ourselves studying next to each other at the dining room table, but would have to move to different sides to avoid the touches that were so distracting.

Inevitably, my hand would reach out for his or my leg was slide up to touch him and we'd smile at each other. Eventually, one of us would get up and take their books to the bedroom and close the door.

It was the only way we could get anything done, but after we had completed our work, we fell into each other's arms and made love.

After my last exam, I was confident that I had managed a fourth straight semester with a 4.0 GPA and much of it was thanks to Jimmie, for supporting me and being strong, forcing me to study and work when the only thing I wanted to do was feel his body against mine.

During the week after finals, but before our wedding, Jimmie had his bachelor's party and I had my wedding shower.

For Jimmie, he refused to do anything more than agree to meet the guys for a night at the pub. Jeff told me later that they rented a private room and played poker, smoked cigars, and drank until nearly sunrise.

Maria arranged my wedding shower and hosted at her family's home. Her aunt made the absolutely most incredible Filipino food for us, many dishes I hadn't even seen before.

When it came time to open gifts from all of my girlfriends, a pretty consistent theme became apparent. Almost all of the gifts were very much for Jimmie, not for me, as I opened box after box of skimpy lingerie. Perhaps I would have to seduce him again on our honeymoon.

For our last night together before driving to the shore, Jimmie ran a hot bath for me that smelled of roses, with what must have been dozens of candles lighting the bathroom.

I finally emerged from the spa he had made for me to find that he had placed candles around the entire apartment and dinner was waiting for me on the table.

We made love that night, the last time before I would be his wife and he would be my husband.

———————

I watched in awe as we drove across the bridge to Ocean City, on a barrier island off the coast of the Eastern Shore. Tomorrow was my wedding, our wedding. It was so close now.

At our hotel, Jimmie and I had separate rooms. It was so odd to me that we would be staying apart for even one night, the first night since I had told him that I still loved him in fact, but we were both just old fashioned enough to want to maintain that tradition.

After carrying our things up to our rooms, he kissed me and told me he'd be waiting downstairs in the bar.

I took a wonderful hot shower and stood before the mirror doing my hair in an intricate braid. I wanted to be perfect for him, for every moment I would be with him.

I remembered that first night after I had graduated from high school and him from college. I'd fallen asleep on the sofa and he didn't recognize me at first. Then his eyes had wandered on my body and he'd made me feel like a woman for the first time in my life.

As I slid into my dress, my body felt the warmth of his eyes on me.

When I finally deemed myself ready for him, I slipped into my sandals and made my way downstairs. I found him, as promised, in the bar.

Before he could see me, I stopped to admire him, wearing a pair of slacks that I absolutely loved on him and a blazer that I knew emphasized his trim waist and broad shoulders when he buttoned it.

He was leaning on the bar with his elbow, his chin resting on his hand, looking very pensive. He turned and looked at me, his hand dropping to the bar with a thud as he slid off his stool, standing to meet me. As soon as I was within reach, I took his hand.

I could feel his strength as he took me into his arms. His lips pressed to mine and I was thankful that he was holding me up, as I melted in his embrace. Before pulling away, he whispered in my ear, "You're absolutely incredible."

I had no words to tell him what he means to me.

When we arrived at the restaurant for our rehearsal dinner, Jeff was waiting out front. Maria and Mia had been so important for me during the wedding planning, helping with dresses, flowers, invitations, and more, but Jeff had gone above and beyond with his support for us. Every decision that we made, he made sure it happened. He is a brother to both of us.

After greeting us both with hugs, he lead us inside. He asked us to wait just outside of where our rehearsal dinner was and said we'd know when to come inside.

I looked up at Jimmie, so completely filled with happiness, while we waited. I silently counted the hours until we would be married in my head.

Suddenly, I heard applause. Jimmie smiled at me and we walked in together.

The night was a complete blur, as our most loved friends talked and laughed with us. Dinner was wonderful, a truly Maryland affair with blue crab, corn, and other local dishes.

For the entire evening, pictures of Jimmie and I cycled on a TV screen on the wall from a slideshow that Mia had arranged. There were moments that were so vivid in my memory: Jimmie and I posing at the pub the first time I met Jeff, a picture Jimmie had taken of our smiling faces that I knew was from when we were in bed a few weeks ago, and a picture of the two of

us surrounded by people, moments after we had announced our engagement to the world.

Occasionally, pictures of our childhood would appear, Jimmie looking so much older and more mature than me, even in his awkward teenage years. Pictures of myself, younger than I could even remember, floated in front of my eyes. I stopped breathing for a moment when a picture appeared of us, Jimmie with his arms around me. I must have been maybe 11 or 12 and he was a young man. He still held me like he was protecting me from the world.

There were also spectacular pictures that I had never seen before that caused me to gasp. In one, we were standing in the hallway and I was holding my violin at my side as Jimmie's fingers gently tilted my head up to him. It must have been the moment just before he kissed me after my last concert. In another, I was sitting next to Jimmie as he slid my ring onto my finger. Jimmie had asked for Jeff's help that day. I had no idea that he had taken that

picture of us. I would always have that moment in my mind, but now I had the most incredible picture of it.

So many of the pictures brought tears to my eyes as the memories flooded through me. I would stare at Jimmie in awe after a new picture appeared and he would smile and kiss me on the cheek.

I was admiring a picture of the two of us at an Orioles game when I completely froze. A knot overtook my stomach and my throat closed so that I couldn't breathe.

"Jimmie..."

"Sharon, what is it?"

My lips trembled as mom stood in the room looking at us. We hadn't seen her since that night, my concert, our engagement.

I wasn't even thinking as I started to rise to my feet. I felt Jimmie's hand on my leg, pushing me back to my chair, and I turned to look up at him.

"Let me."

His hand rested on my shoulder as he stood next to me. As soon as he was out of reach, Mia sat in his seat and moved close to me. Maria was on my other side. They each took one of my hands and squeezed.

Mom...

I watched as Jimmie and mom left the room together.

Horrible, terrible thoughts of something happening to prevent us from getting married ran rampant through my mind.

I looked at Maria, then Mia. I wondered if my face matched the look of shock on theirs. I knew that they were talking to me, but I couldn't hear a word they were saying. My eyes were locked on the door, waiting for Jimmie.

I don't know how long it took, but the door finally opened and I saw Jimmie again. He had a look of determination on his face. As

he approached me, his eyes never left mine and he softened into a gentle smile.

He came around the table and held out his arm. I cautiously slipped my hand into his, still terrified, but somewhat reassured, first by his demeanor and then by his touch. He lead me outside and I pressed as close to him as I could.

Outside, Jimmie turned and I saw her again. She was crying.

Every □uestion ran wild in my mind. Why are you here? Did you come to try and talk us out of getting married? Why can't you support us, be happy for us?

"Mom..."

He eyes met mine.

"Savannah, honey, I'm so sorry."

I'm sorry, too, mom. I just want you to be happy for us.

Tears ran down her cheeks.

I felt Jimmie next to me, his lips near my ear.

"It's okay."

He wouldn't tell me it was okay if it wasn't. His hand briefly squeezed mine and then let go. Mom, are you here for us?

I took a step forward and felt mom's arms slide around me. I crumpled into her embrace.

"I'm so sorry, baby girl. I love you. Please forgive me. I want you to be happy. I want you to... be with Jimmie."

Mom...

My emotions overwhelmed me and I cried. She had come back to us. She wanted us to be happy, together. She held me tightly and we cried together, reunited.

As she held me, she told me how sorry she was for what she had done. She said that was selfish and put herself before us, but

she would never do that again. Our happiness was her only thought now.

She talked to me and soothed me. She would be there for our wedding. After I said, "I do," I would look back and she would be smiling for us.

I could barely process everything. I had been completely prepared to be married without her there. For months, my family was Jimmie and our friends.

I don't know if other people would accept the situation the way Jimmie and I did. We never wanted her out of our lives, but it was the way it had to be until she came around. Once she did, we wouldn't think of anything other than having her there to share with us. That was all that mattered.

For the rest of the evening, it was hard to believe that everyone I loved was there with me, with us. Whenever it felt like a dream, I sat next to mom and rested my hand on her arm. She was real.

She watched as pictures of Jimmie and I flashed on the screen and we told her the story of us.

When she said goodbye, she promised that she would see us get married. I held her tightly to me, remembering all of the years when her embrace had been my comfort.

Later, I stood in front of Jimmie in the lobby of our hotel.

"I'm so happy she's here."

His voice was soft and kind, "I am, too. She should share this with us."

I pressed my face to his chest.

"Jimmie, I love you."

I pulled away so that I could look into his eyes and trace my fingers along his cheek.

"My husband..."

He bent down and kissed me, gently and with all of the love that existed between us.

"My wife... my Sharon."

It was so hard to let him go, my only comfort being that the time before we would be married was now measured in hours.

How I slept, I have no idea.

I awoke into a blur.

As soon as I texted Mia and Maria to let them know I was awake, they were knocking on my door, demanding to come in. We immediately hugged and giggled.

It was finally here. My day. Our day.

The three of us went to the hotel's spa as planned and sat chatting and reminiscing as we were pampered to within an inch of melting into happy little puddles with manicures, pedicures, massages, and baths. My fingers and toes were painted, brightly red for Maryland, and the stylist used so little makeup that I couldn't even feel anything on my face, but when I

turned to the mirror, I wondered if the beautiful woman who stared back at me was the same woman that Jimmie had always seen when he looked at me.

The hair stylist on staff begged me to let her do something with my hair, even offering her services for free. She said that she had never had a bride with such long and full hair, but I politely refused. On this day, of all days, I would wear my hair completely free for Jimmie.

After returning to my room, I had a few minutes to myself.

I stood on my balcony, listening to the ocean waves breaking on the beach under the magnificent sky. I breathed deeply, smelling the clean, salty air.

I think a part of me always knew that this is where I had to be in life. From the time I was brought into his home, Jimmie was my world. He had protected me and cared for me, always supportive, always there for me.

When I shed my awkward, girlish appearance, I finally had the courage to seek out his love. We spent a summer together and it was as if we had spent a lifetime together. Even before my mind knew what I wanted, my heart needed him.

I had kissed him. In a single moment, our lives changed. It wasn't even really a conscious decision, it had been my heart guiding me to the love of my life.

He didn't reject me. He wasn't angry at me. He returned my love and held me in his arms. My life, our lives, were forever better.

I heard a knock on the door and paused for one last breath before turning to answer.

Maria □uietly stepped in, "It's time."

I pulled her to me and hugged her.

"Thank you, for everything. I wouldn't be who I am without you."

She whispered back, "Mahal kita, Ineng."

Minutes later, we were with Mia and driving south to Assateague. I rolled down my window and held my hand outside, changing the angles to let it flow through the wind. I had once felt so overwhelmed by life, consumed by loss and sadness, but now Jimmie had brought love to me and I felt like my hand, floating on invisible air currents that lifted me away from all that had weighed me down.

Gone were the fears, the worries, the trepidation. It was my wedding day and as I watched the ocean through my window, I was entirely focused on the present and the future.

Mia pulled her car into a parking lot and the three of us walked to the beach, where two tents stood, starkly white against the deep blue of the ocean and the crisp azure of the sky. We chatted and giggled, lost in anticipation of coming events.

Maria and Mia took my things into one tent, but I took a few moments for myself, wandering among the chairs on the sand. A

trellis was placed in front of the chairs, forming a window to the ocean beyond. I smiled as I ran my fingers along the white roses woven into the structure. It was simple and beautiful. It was to be the most sacred place in my life, where I promised to spend my life with Jimmie and he would become my husband.

I walked further onto the beach, until my feet touched the moist sand where the strongest waves had broken and run uphill before sliding back to rejoin the ocean. Instead of the soft pools that my feet left behind in the dry sand behind me, my feet now left clearly defined imprints. A few strides later and I watched as cool water chased up the beach and flowed over my toes. I stood still and let the receding wave pull the sand out from under my feet.

I closed my eyes and felt the ocean, the sand, and the gentle breeze caress my skin. I breathed deeply and could feel my hand slide into his. My lips curled into a soft smile, before widening as my joy consumed me.

I took my moment and then turned and saw Mia and Maria waiting for me up the beach. Soon, I was inside my tent, preparing for Jimmie.

Maria stood behind me, brushing my hair. Mia dug around inside of her bag before moving to sit in front of me.

"Savannah, Maria and I both love you so much. We know this won't match your fingernails and toenails, but we wanted you to have something new and something blue for your wedding day."

She handed me a small beautifully wrapped box. I carefully removed the silver and white paper, then opened the box. Inside was an incredible sapphire pendant. I immediately set the box on the table next to me and stood to embrace both of them.

"You are both my incredible sisters. Thank you. I love you."

We talked and laughed as we took our time changing and getting ready, sharing memories, but also talking about the plans

Jimmie and I had for the future. We knew that we couldn't move to the Eastern Shore as long as Jimmie worked at NASA and I was at Maryland, but maybe Annapolis would be close enough. Maria asked me if I would continue playing after I graduated. I hoped that I would. Max had told me that I could play in any concert hall in the world if I wanted and I could see myself standing in Vienna or Sydney, with Jimmie in the front row.

Eventually, we were ready and I could hear the voices of our guests outside. I stood before my sisters and bowed my head as Maria placed a wreath of baby's breath on my head.

She whispered to me, "You are perfect."

I had to quickly grab a tissue to dry my eyes.

Mia poked her head out of the tent and asked Sarabeth to come inside. She was a friend from several music classes and Jimmie and I had asked her to play for our wedding. After she came inside, holding

her violin at her side, she thanked me for including her and complimented both myself and my dress. We had worked together on an arrangement for both the processional and recessional and she had impressed me with her dedication to ensuring it was perfect.

Again, Mia looked outside and I heard her briefly speaking with Jeff. She closed the opening and came to me.

"Are you ready?"

"Completely."

She smiled at me and she, Mia, and Sarabeth took their places. I stayed to the side, out of sight, as they tied open the flaps.

Sara beth stepped out and after a moment, I heard her beginning the arrangement we had created of "All of Me". She played beautifully, turning an already lovely piano ballad into a gorgeous classical love song.

Mia handed me my bou□uet of white calla lilies and then stopped at the opening before stepping out into the fading sunlight. I couldn't help counting the beats in my head as she disappeared and Maria followed her, stepping lightly at the appropriate times.

I moved forward and breathed deeply, deliberately. One last time, I ran my fingers over my engagement ring. It would always be paired with my wedding band from now on.

A smile spread across my face and I stepped into the light.

Immediately, my eyes locked onto Jimmie. I had to catch my breath with every step, as I moved closer and closer to him.

He was unbelievably handsome. The sun behind me cast long shadows across our guests from the tents, but he stood bathed in the oranges and reds of the sunset, framed by the deepening blue of the sky behind him. He wore simple white linen pants, which flapped slowly in the breeze,

and a wonderfully fitted red dress shirt, untucked and with his sleeves rolled up to his elbows. Like me, his feet were bare and sunk into the sand.

He looked so relaxed, but his eyes were completely focused on me and his broad smile invited me to him.

It took an eternity for me to reach him, but when I did, I handed my bou□uet to Maria and he took my hand. His touch sent my heart pounding in my chest. I wanted to brush my fingers along the smooth skin of his cheek, trace the outline of his jaw, and pull him to me. His fingers gently caressed mine and and I took a small step closer to him, so that my arm could just barely press against his.

I was lost in his eyes, so blue in the fading light, as our ceremony began.

"Friends and family, thank you for coming today to celebrate in the marriage of Michael and Savannah."

My eyes briefly left Jimmie, just long enough to see mom sitting in the first row, before returning to focus on him, the love of my life.

"You have gathered here to share in their commitment to each other and to offer your love and support as they begin their lives together, as husband and wife."

My husband...

"Every person travels a unique path in life, seeking meaning and purpose, affection and companionship. Our path as are often filled with successes and failures, both of which create who we are as individuals and eventually contribute to who we become as partners."

We would have so many more successes in the future. Whatever successes lay ahead, we would achieve them together and none would be as important as pledging our lives to each other, building a family together.

"Michael's path has taken him from his home here on the Eastern Shore, to

incredible successes in education, his career, and life. He has traveled across the ocean and into the farthest reaches of the universe inquiring into a deeper knowledge of the world around us and an understanding of the significance of life. He will continue exploring in the years and decades to come, yet he will always return home, to where his heart belongs, with Savannah."

I beamed at him, so proud of all that he was and would be.

"Savannah's path has carried her from the shy girl of her youth to the incredible woman that stands before you today. Her life has been defined by the interweaving of her love for science and her passion for music. She has achieved the highest honors in education and dazzled audiences with the enthusiasm for life that she expresses through her violin. Wherever she may go, to concert halls around the world or a laboratory here in Maryland, she will continue bringing together the elements of life that she loves, with Michael by her side."

I s□ueezed his hand.

I will always be by your side.

"For Michael and Savannah, their paths, as incredible as they have been apart, could only ever lead to each other and to the joining of their lives into a single path forward, together."

Forward, to careers, a home... family.

"In making this formal commitment, Michael and Savannah pledge to each other and to you that throughout friendship and faults ,companionship and struggle, their love will serve as a guiding influence, forever bringing them together, always on a single path."

I tried to hold back my tears as emotions flooded through me, most of all, my pure and unlimited love for Jimmie.

"And now, Michael and Savannah would like to make their vows to each other, for all here to witness."

I felt my lips trembling as I remembered the words I had written for Jimmie. I took his hands in mine and stared up into his eyes.

"Jimmie... my dear Jimmie. You are the love of my life and my inspiration. Every day I live is a day that I seek your love and friendship. Everything that we have been through has made us the people that we are today and I accept all of it without any reservation, because now I stand before you on our wedding day."

My lips began to fail me and my voice wavered. No, no... a little more, don't fall apart yet.

"I will always be by your side, providing you joy and comfort. I pledge to you my love and support, for every day of my life..."

I couldn't continue as I was completely overcome and I struggled to say the most important words in my life.

"I love you."

My eyes were blurry with tears and I s□ueezed them closed, feeling wetness running down my face. I felt Jimmie lift my hands and press his lips to my fingers. I opened my eyes and was immersed in my love for him.

Jimmie's voice was strong and clear.

"My wonderful Sharon. You are absolutely everything to me and all that I need in the world. I live and die with your smile and your touch. I need you beside me for the rest of my life, as my best friend... my companion."

Oh, Jimmie...

"I am overwhelmed when I think about the ways that our relationship has changed over the years, all of the experiences that we have shared and the times when you rescued me from my absolute darkest moments. I was completely lost without you and I am so incredibly thankful that

you have chosen to spend your life with me."

It was never a choice. I need you.

"The only thing that can possibly compare to my love for you is my admiration for the incredible person that you have become. I am in complete awe of all that you are, my perfect Sharon. Every part of me strives to ensure that I never disappoint you, that I never let you down in any way."

His hands held mine steady.

" You are the love of my life. I pledge to you my love and support, for every day of my life. I will comfort you and cherish you, protect you and nurture you, always. On this day, I give my life to you. I love you."

I watched, through teary eyes, as his face showed pure love for me.

A voice, "May I have the rings?"

I was barely aware of anything other than Jimmie.

"These rings will serve as an abiding symbol of the love and union between Michael and Savannah."

I reached out and took his ring in my trembling fingers. His hand steadied mine as I slid his wedding band onto his finger. I watched as it passed over his knuckle to its final resting place.

I looked back down as I felt Jimmie place my ring on my finger. He carefully slid it until it rested against my engagement ring. My eyes moved back to his as more tears streamed down my cheeks.

"Savannah, do you take Michael to stand by your side from this day forward, as your lawfully wedded husband?"

I could barely whisper, "I do."

"Michael, do you take Savannah to stand by your side from this day forward, as your lawfully wedded wife?"

Despite the moisture in his eyes, his voice remained firm and sure.

"I do."

"I now pronounce you, in the eyes of all here and the State of Maryland, husband and wife."

I moved closer to him.

"You may..."

I heard nothing else.

My lips pressed to Jimmie's, my husband.